Boy in a Blue Pullover

Ruskin Bond is known for his signature simplistic and witty writing style. He is the author of several bestselling short stories, novellas, collections, essays and children's books; and has contributed a number of poems and articles to various magazines and anthologies. At the age of twenty-three, he won the prestigious John Llewellyn Rhys Prize for his first novel, *The Room on the Roof*. He was also the recipient of the Padma Shri in 1999, Lifetime Achievement Award by the Delhi Government in 2012, and the Padma Bhushan in 2014.

Born in 1934, Ruskin Bond grew up in Jamnagar, Shimla, New Delhi and Dehradun. Apart from three years in the UK, he has spent all his life in India, and now lives in Landour, Mussoorie, with his adopted family.

RUSKIN BOND
Boy in a Blue Pullover

Published by
Rupa Publications India Pvt. Ltd 2020
7/16, Ansari Road, Daryaganj
New Delhi 110002

Sales centres:
Allahabad Bengaluru Chennai
Hyderabad Jaipur Kathmandu
Kolkata Mumbai

Copyright © Ruskin Bond 2020

This is a work of fiction. Names, characters, places and incidents are either the product of the author's imagination or are used fictitiously and any resemblance to any actual person, living or dead, events or locales is entirely coincidental.

All rights reserved.
No part of this publication may be reproduced, transmitted, or stored in a retrieval system, in any form or by any means, electronic, mechanical, photocopying, recording or otherwise, without the prior permission of the publisher.

ISBN: 978-93-5333-831-2

First impression 2020

10 9 8 7 6 5 4 3 2 1

Printed at HT Media Ltd, Greater Noida

This book is sold subject to the condition that it shall not, by way of trade or otherwise, be lent, resold, hired out, or otherwise circulated, without the publisher's prior consent, in any form of binding or cover other than that in which it is published.

CONTENTS

Introduction	vii
1. Friends of My Youth	1
2. And Now We Are Twelve	7
3. Come Roaming With Me	16
4. Children of India	17
5. Our Local Team	23
6. Spell Broken	25
7. Simply Living	26
8. Boy in a Blue Pullover	47
9. Garhwal Himalaya	48
10. A Song of Many Rivers	50
11. Adventures in Reading	66
12. My Far Pavilions	74
13. Joyfully I Write	78
14. To Light a Fire	85
15. The India I Carried with Me	86

16.	Midwinter, Deserted Hill Station	97
17.	His Last Words	98
18.	The Prospect of Flowers	99
19.	Angry River	107
20.	Grandfather Fights an Ostrich	133
21.	The Blue Umbrella	137
22.	The Cherry Tree	159
23.	Susanna's Seven Husbands	165
24.	Hassan, the Baker	171
25.	Gracie	177
26.	Dinner with Foster	191
27.	Remember this Day	200
28.	An Evening at the Savoy with H.H.	204

INTRODUCTION

By and large, I suppose, writers have to stay in the plains to make a living. Hill people have their work cut out just trying to wrest a livelihood from the stony soil. And as for mountaineers, they climb their peaks and move on, in search of other peaks; they seldom take up residence in the mountains.

But to me, as a writer, mountains have been kind. They were kind from the beginning, when I threw up a job in Delhi and rented a small cottage on the outskirts of a hill station. Today, most hill stations are rich men's playgrounds, but all those years ago, they were places where people of modest means could live quite cheaply. There were very few cars and everyone walked about.

The cottage was situated on the edge of an oak and maple forest and I spent many years in it, most of them happy years, writing stories, essays, poems, books for children. It was only after I came to live in the hills that I began writing for children. The stories that we read as children are the ones that stay with us all our lives.

For over several decades now, I have been living in this rather raffish hill station, and when people ask me why, I usually say 'I forgot to go away.' But that is only partly true. I have had good times here, and bad, and the good times have predominated. There's something to be said for a place if you've been happy there, and it's nice to be able to record some of the events and people that made for fun and happy living.

The stories, novellas, anecdotes and reminiscences in this collection deal with the lighter and, at times, nostalgic side of life in the hill station and around it. Over the years, Mussoorie has changed a little, but not too much. I have changed too, but not too much. And I think I'm a better person for having spent more than half my life up here.

Ruskin Bond

FRIENDS OF MY YOUTH

Friendship is all about doing things together. It may be climbing a mountain, fishing in a mountain stream, cycling along a country road, camping in a forest clearing, or simply travelling together and sharing the experiences that a new place can bring.

On at least two of these counts, Sudheer qualified as a friend, albeit a troublesome one, given to involving me in his adolescent escapades.

I met him in Dehra soon after my return from England. He turned up at my room, saying he'd heard I was a writer and did I have any comics to lend him?

'I don't write comics,' I said; but there were some comics lying around, left over from my own boyhood collection so I gave these to the lanky youth who stood smiling in the doorway, and he thanked me and said he'd bring them back. From my window I saw him cycling off in the general direction of Dalanwala.

He turned up again a few days later and dumped a large pile of new-looking comics on my desk. 'Here are all the latest,' he announced. 'You can keep them for me. I'm not allowed to read comics at home.'

It was only weeks later that I learnt he was given to pilfering comics and magazines from the town's bookstores. In no time at all, I'd become a receiver of stolen goods!

My landlady had warned me against Sudheer and so had one or two others. He had acquired a certain notoriety for having been expelled from his school. He had been in charge of the library, and before a consignment of newly-acquired books could be registered and library stamped, he had sold them back to the bookshop from which they had originally been purchased. Very enterprising but not to be countenanced in a very pukka public school. He was now studying in a municipal school too poor to afford a library.

Sudheer was an amoral scamp all right, but I found it difficult to avoid him, or to resist his undeniable and openly affectionate manner. He could make you laugh. And anyone who can do that is easily forgiven for a great many faults.

One day he produced a couple of white mice from his pockets and left them on my desk.

'You keep them for me,' he said. 'I'm not allowed to keep them at home.'

There were a great many things he was not allowed to keep at home. Anyway, the white mice were given a home in an old cupboard, where my landlady kept unwanted dishes, pots and pans, and they were quite happy there, being fed on bits of bread or chapatti, until one day I heard shrieks from the storeroom, and charging into it, found my dear stout landlady having hysterics as one of the white mice sought refuge under her blouse and the other ran frantically up and down her back.

Sudheer had to find another home for the white mice. It was that, or finding another home for myself.

Most young men, boys, and quite a few girls used bicycles.

There was a cycle hire shop across the road, and Sudheer persuaded me to hire cycles for both of us. We cycled out of town, through tea gardens and mustard fields, and down a forest road until we discovered a small, shallow river where we bathed and wrestled on the sand. Although I was three or four years older than Sudheer, he was much the stronger, being about six foot tall and broad in the shoulders. His parents had come from Bhanu, a rough and ready district on the North West Frontier, as a result of the partition of the country. His father ran a small press situated behind the sabzi mandi and brought out a weekly newspaper called *The Frontier Times*.

We came to the stream quite often. It was Sudheer's way of playing truant from school without being detected in the bazaar or at the cinema. He was sixteen when I met him, and eighteen when we parted, but I can't recall that he ever showed any interest in his schoolwork.

He took me to his home in the Karanpur bazaar, then a stronghold of the Bhanu community. The Karanpur boys were an aggressive lot and resented Sudheer's friendship with an angrez. To avoid a confrontation, I would use the back alleys and side streets to get to and from the house in which they lived.

Sudheer had been overindulged by his mother, who protected him from his father's wrath. Both parents felt I might have an 'improving' influence on their son, and encouraged our friendship. His elder sister seemed more doubtful. She felt he was incorrigible, beyond redemption, and that I was not much better, and she was probably right.

The father invited me to his small press and asked me if I'd like to work with him. I agreed to help with the newspaper for a couple of hours every morning. This involved proofreading and editing news agency reports. Uninspiring work, but useful.

Meanwhile, Sudheer had got hold of a pet monkey, and he

carried it about in the basket attached to the handlebar of his bicycle. He used it to ingratiate himself with the girls. 'How sweet! How pretty!' they would exclaim, and Sudheer would get the monkey to show them its tricks.

After some time, however, the monkey appeared to be infected by Sudheer's amorous nature, and would make obscene gestures which were not appreciated by his former admirers. On one occasion, the monkey made off with a girl's dupatta. A chase ensued, and the dupatta retrieved, but the outcome of it all was that Sudheer was accosted by the girl's brothers and given a black eye and a bruised cheek. His father took the monkey away and returned it to the itinerant juggler who had sold it to the young man.

Sudheer soon developed an insatiable need for money. He wasn't getting anything at home, apart from what he pinched from his mother and sister, and his father urged me not to give the boy any money. After paying for my boarding and lodging I had very little to spare, but Sudheer seemed to sense when a money order or cheque arrived, and would hang around, spinning tall tales of great financial distress until, in order to be rid of him, I would give him five to ten rupees. (In those days, a magazine payment seldom exceeded fifty rupees.)

He was becoming something of a trial, constantly interrupting me in my work, and even picking up confectionery from my landlady's small shop and charging it to my account.

I had stopped going for bicycle rides. He had wrecked one of the cycles and the shopkeeper held me responsible for repairs.

The sad thing was that Sudheer had no other friends. He did not go in for team games or for music or other creative pursuits which might have helped him to move around with people of his own age group. He was a loner with a propensity for mischief. Had he entered a bicycle race, he would have won easily. Forever eluding a variety of pursuers, he was extremely fast on his bike. But we did not have cycle races in Dehra.

And then, for a blessed two or three weeks, I saw nothing of my unpredictable friend.

I discovered later, that he had taken a fancy to a young schoolteacher, about five years his senior, who lived in a hostel up at Rajpur. His cycle rides took him in that direction. As usual, his charm proved irresistible, and it wasn't long before the teacher and the acolyte were taking rides together down lonely forest roads. This was all right by me, of course, but it wasn't the norm with the middle-class matrons of small-town India, at least not in 1957. Hostel wardens, other students, and naturally Sudheer's parents, were all in a state of agitation. So I wasn't surprised when Sudheer turned up in my room to announce that he was on his way to Nahan, to study at an inter-college there.

Nahan was a small hill town about sixty miles from Dehra. Sudheer was banished to the home of his mama, an uncle who was a sub-inspector in the local police force. He had promised to see that Sudheer stayed out of trouble.

Whether he succeeded or not, I could not tell, for a couple of months later I gave up my rooms in Dehra and left for Delhi. I lost touch with Sudheer's family, and it was only several years later, when I bumped into an old acquaintance, that I was given news of my erstwhile friend.

He had apparently done quite well for himself. Taking off for Calcutta, he had used his charm and his fluent English to land a job as an assistant on a tea estate. Here he had proved quite efficient, earning the approval of his manager and employers. But his roving eyes soon got him into trouble. The women working in the tea gardens became prey to his amorous and amoral nature. Keeping one mistress was acceptable. Keeping several was asking for trouble. He was found dead, early one morning, with his throat cut.

AND NOW WE ARE TWELVE

People often ask me why I've chosen to live in Mussoorie for so long—almost forty years without any significant breaks.

'I forgot to go away,' I tell them, but of course, that isn't the real reason.

The people here are friendly, but then people are friendly in a great many other places. The hills, the valleys are beautiful; but they are just as beautiful in Kulu or Kumaon.

'This is where the family has grown up and where we all live,' I say, and those who don't know me are puzzled because the general impression of the writer is of a reclusive old bachelor.

Unmarried I may be, but single I am not. Not since Prem came to live and work with me in 1970. A year later, he was married. Then his children came along and stole my heart; and when they grew up, their children came along and stole my wits. So now I'm an enchanted bachelor, head of a family of twelve. Sometimes I go out to bat, sometimes to bowl, but generally I prefer to be twelfth man, carrying out the drinks!

In the old days, when I was a solitary writer living on baked beans, the prospect of my suffering from obesity was very remote. Now there is a little more of author than there used to be, and the other day five-year-old Gautam patted me on my tummy (or balcony, as I prefer to call it) and remarked, 'Dada, you should join the WWF.'

'I'm already a member,' I said, 'I joined the World Wildlife Fund years ago.'

'Not that,' he said. 'I mean the World Wrestling Federation.'

If I have a tummy today, it's thanks to Gautam's grandfather and now his mother who, over the years, have made sure that I am well-fed and well-proportioned.

Forty years ago, when I was a lean young man, people would look at me and say, 'Poor chap, he's definitely undernourished. What on earth made him take up writing as a profession?' Now they look at me and say, 'You wouldn't think he was a writer, would you? Too well nourished!'

◆

It was a cold, wet and windy March evening when Prem came back from the village with his wife and first-born child, then just four months old. In those days, they had to walk to the house from the bus stand; it was a half-hour walk in the cold rain, and the baby was all wrapped up when they entered the front room. Finally, I got a glimpse of him, and he of me, and it was friendship at first sight. Little Rakesh (as he was to be called) grabbed me by the nose and held on. He did not have much of a nose to grab, but he had a dimpled chin and I played with it until he smiled.

The little chap spent a good deal of his time with me during those first two years of his in Maplewood—learning to crawl, to toddle, and then to walk unsteadily about the little sitting-room. I would carry him into the garden, and later, up the steep gravel path to the main road. Rakesh enjoyed these little excursions, and so did I, because in pointing out trees, flowers, birds, butterflies, beetles, grasshoppers, et al, I was giving myself a chance to observe them better instead of just taking them for granted.

In particular, there was a pair of squirrels that lived in the big oak tree outside the cottage. Squirrels are rare in Mussoorie though common enough down in the valley. This couple must have come up for the summer. They became quite friendly, and although they never got around to taking food from our hands, they were soon entering the house quite freely. The sitting room window opened directly on to the oak tree whose various denizens—ranging from stag-beetles to small birds and even an acrobatic bat—took to darting in and out of the cottage at various times of the day or night.

Life at Maplewood was quite idyllic, and when Rakesh's baby brother, Suresh, came into the world, it seemed we were all set for a long period of domestic bliss; but at such times tragedy is often lurking just around the corner. Suresh was just over a year old when he contracted tetanus. Doctors and hospitals were of no avail. He suffered—as any child would from this terrible affliction—and left this world before he had a chance of getting to know it. His parents were broken-hearted. And I feared for Rakesh, for he wasn't a very healthy boy, and two of his cousins in the village had already succumbed to tuberculosis.

It was to be a difficult year for me. A criminal charge was brought against me for a slightly risque story I'd written for a Bombay magazine. I had to face trial in Bombay and this involved three journeys there over a period of a year and a half, before an irate but perceptive judge found the charges baseless and gave me an honourable acquittal.

It's the only time I've been involved with the law and I sincerely hope it is the last. Most cases drag on interminably, and the main beneficiaries are the lawyers. My trial would have been much longer had not the prosecutor died of a heart attack in the middle of the proceedings. His successor did not pursue it with the same vigour. His heart was not in it. The whole issue had started with a complaint by a local politician, and when he lost interest so did the prosecution. Nevertheless the trial, once begun, had to be seen through. The defence (organized by the concerned magazine) marshalled its witnesses (which included Nissim Ezekiel and the Marathi playwright Vijay Tendulkar). I made a short speech which couldn't have been very memorable as I have forgotten it! And everyone, including the judge, was bored with the whole business. After that, I steered clear of controversial publications. I have never set out to shock the world. Telling a meaningful story was all that really mattered. And that is still the case.

I was looking forward to continuing our idyllic existence in Maplewood, but it was not to be. The powers-that-be, in the shape of the Public Works Department (PWD), had decided to build a 'strategic' road just below the cottage and without any warning to us, all the trees in the vicinity were felled (including the friendly old oak) and the hillside was rocked by explosives and bludgeoned by bulldozers. I decided it was time to move. Prem and Chandra (Rakesh's mother) wanted to move too; not because of the road, but because they associated the house with the death of little Suresh, whose presence seemed to haunt every room, every corner of the cottage. His little cries of pain and suffering still echoed through the still hours of the night.

I rented rooms at the top of Landour, a good thousand feet higher up the mountain. Rakesh was now old enough to go to school, and every morning I would walk with him down to the little convent school near the clock tower. Prem would go to fetch him in the afternoon. The walk took us about half-an hour, and on the way Rakesh would ask for a story and I would have to rack my brains in order to invent one. I am not the most inventive of writers, and fantastical plots are beyond me. My forte is observation, recollection, and reflection. Small boys prefer action. So I invented a leopard who suffered from acute indigestion because he'd eaten one human too many and a belt buckle was causing an obstruction.

This went down quite well until Rakesh asked me how the leopard got around the problem of the victim's clothes.

'The secret,' I said, 'is to pounce on them when their trousers are off!'

Not the stuff of which great picture books are made, but then, I've never attempted to write stories for beginners. Red Riding Hood's granny-eating wolf always scared me as a small boy, and yet parents have always found it acceptable for toddlers. Possibly they feel grannies are expendable.

Mukesh was born around this time and Savitri (Dolly) a couple of years later. When Dolly grew older, she was annoyed at having been named Savitri (my choice), which is now considered very old-fashioned; so we settled for Dolly. I can understand a child's dissatisfaction with given names.

My first name was Owen, which in Welsh means 'brave'. As I am not in the least brave, I have preferred not to use it. One given name and one surname should be enough.

When my granny said, 'But you should try to be brave, otherwise how will you survive in this cruel world?' I replied: 'Don't worry, I can run very fast.'

Not that I've ever had to do much running, except when I was pursued by a lissome Australian lady who thought I'd make a good obedient husband. It wasn't so much the lady I was running from, but the prospect of spending the rest of my life in some remote cattle station in the Australian outback.

Anyone who has tried to drag me away from India has always met with stout resistance.

◆

Up on the heights of Landour lived a motley crowd. My immediate neighbours included a Frenchwoman who played the sitar (very badly) all through the night; a Spanish lady with two husbands. One of whom practised acupuncture—rather ineffectively as far as he was concerned, for he seemed to be dying of some mysterious debilitating disease. The other came and went rather mysteriously, and finally ended up in Tihar Jail, having been apprehended at Delhi airport carrying a large amount of contraband hashish.

Apart from these and a few other colourful characters, the area was inhabited by some very respectable people, retired brigadiers, air marshals and rear admirals, almost all of whom were busy writing their memoirs. I had to read or listen to extracts from their literary efforts. This was slow torture. A few years before, I had done a stint of editing for a magazine called *Imprint*. It had involved going through hundreds of badly written manuscripts, and in some cases (friends of the owner!) rewriting some of them for publication. One of life's joys had been to throw up that particular job, and now here I was, besieged by all the top brass of the Army, Navy and Air Force, each one determined that I should read, inwardly digest, improve, and if possible find a publisher for their outpourings.

Thank goodness they were all retired. I could not be shot or court-martialled. But at least two of them set their wives upon me, and these intrepid ladies would turn up around noon with my 'homework'—typescripts to read and edit! There was no escape. My own writing was of no consequence to them. I told them that I was taking sitar lessons, but they disapproved, saying I was more suited to the tabla.

When Prem discovered a set of vacant rooms further down the Landour slope, close to school and bazaar, I rented them without hesitation. This was Ivy Cottage. Come up and see me sometimes, but leave your manuscripts behind.

When we came to Ivy Cottage in 1980, we were six, Dolly having just been born. Now, twenty-four years later, we are twelve. I think that's a reasonable expansion. The increase has been brought about by Rakesh's marriage twelve years ago, and Mukesh's marriage two years ago. Both precipitated themselves into marriage when they were barely twenty, and both were lucky. Beena and Binita, who happen to be real sisters, have brightened and enlivened our lives with their happy, positive natures and the wonderful children they have brought into the world. More about them later.

Ivy Cottage has, on the whole, been kind to us, and particularly kind to me. Some houses like their occupants, others don't. Maplewood, set in the shadow of the hill lacked a natural cheerfulness; there was a settled gloom about the place. The house at the top of Landour was too exposed to the elements to have any sort of character. The wind moaning in the deodars may have inspired the sitar player but it did nothing for my writing. I produced very little up there.

On the other hand, Ivy Cottage—especially my little room facing the sunrise—has been conducive to creative work. Novellas, poems, essays, children's stories, anthologies, have all come tumbling on to whatever sheets of paper happen to be nearest me. As I write by hand, I have only to grab for the nearest pad, loose sheet, page-proof or envelope whenever the muse takes hold of me, which is surprisingly often.

I came here when I was nearing fifty. Now I'm seventy, and instead of drying up, as some writers do in their later years, I find myself writing with as much ease and assurance as when I was twenty. And I enjoy writing. It's not a burdensome task. I may not have anything of earth-shattering significance to convey to the world, but in conveying my sentiments to you, dear readers, and in telling you something about my relationship with people and the natural world, I hope to bring a little pleasure and sunshine into your life.

Life isn't a bed of roses, not for any of us, and I have never had the comforts or luxuries that wealth can provide. But here I am, doing my own thing, in my own time and my own way. What more can I ask of life? Give me a big cash prize and I'd still be here. I happen to like the view from my window. And I like to have Gautam coming up to me, patting me on the tummy, and telling me that I'll make a good goalkeeper one day.

It's a Sunday morning, as I come to the conclusion of this chapter. There's bedlam in the house. Siddharth's football keeps smashing against the front door. Shrishti is practising her dance routine in the back verandah. Gautam has cut his finger and is trying his best to bandage it with cello tape. He is, of course, the youngest of Rakesh's three musketeers, and probably the most independent-minded. Siddharth, now ten, is restless, never quite able to expend all his energy. 'Does not pay enough attention,' says his teacher. It must be hard for anyone to pay attention in a class of sixty! How does the poor teacher pay attention?

If you, dear reader, have any ambitions to be a writer, you must first rid yourself of any notion that perfect peace and quiet is the first requirement. There is no such thing as perfect peace and quiet except perhaps in a monastery or a cave in the mountains. And what would you write about, living in a cave? One should be able to write in a train, a bus, a bullock-cart, in good weather or bad, on a park bench or in the middle of a noisy classroom.

Of course, the best place is the sun-drenched desk right next to my bed. It isn't always sunny here, but on a good day like this, it's ideal. The children are getting ready for school, dogs are barking in the street, and down near the water tap there's an altercation between two women with empty buckets, the tap having dried up. But these are all background noises and will subside in due course. They are not directed at me.

Hello! Here's Atish, Mukesh's little ten-month-old infant, crawling over the rug, curious to know why I'm sitting on the edge of my bed scribbling away, when I should be playing with him. So I shall play with him for five minutes and then come back to this page. Giving him my time is important. After all, I won't be around when he grows up.

Half-an-hour later. Atish soon tired of playing with me, but meanwhile Gautam had absconded with my pen. When I asked him to return it, he asked, 'Why don't you get a computer? Then we can play games on it.'

'My pen is faster than any computer,' I tell him, 'I wrote three pages this morning without getting out of bed. And yesterday I wrote two pages sitting under Billoo's chestnut tree.'

'Until a chestnut fell on your head,' says Gautam, 'Did it hurt?'

'Only a little,' I said, putting on a brave front.

He had saved the chestnut and now he showed it to me. The smooth brown horse-chestnut shone in the sunlight.

'Let's stick it in the ground,' I said. 'Then in the spring a chestnut tree will come up.'

So we went outside and planted the chestnut on a plot of wasteland. Hopefully a small tree will burst through the earth at about the time this little book is published.

♦

COME ROAMING WITH ME

Out of the city and over the hill,
Into the spaces where time stands still,
Under the tall trees, touching old wood,
Taking the way where warriors once stood;
Crossing the little bridge, losing my way,
But finding a friendly place where I can stay.
Those were the days, friend, when we were strong
And strode down the road to an old marching song
When the dew on the grass was fresh every morn,
And we woke to the call of the ring-dove at dawn.
The years have gone by, and sometimes I falter,
But still I set out for a stroll or a saunter,
For the wind is as fresh as it was in my youth,
And the peach and the pear, still the sweetest of fruit,
So cast away care and come roaming with me,
Where the grass is still green and the air is still free.

CHILDREN OF INDIA

They pass me everyday, on their way to school—boys and girls from the surrounding villages and the outskirts of the hill station. There are no school buses plying for these children; they walk.

For many of them, it's a very long walk to school.

Ranbir, who is ten, has to climb the mountain from his village, four miles distant and 2,000 feet below the town level. He comes in all weathers, wearing the same pair of cheap shoes until they have almost fallen apart.

Ranbir is a cheerful soul. He waves to me whenever he sees me at my window. Sometimes he brings me cucumbers from his father's field. I pay him for the cucumbers; he uses the money for books or for small things needed at home.

Many of the children are like Ranbir—poor, but slightly better off than what their parents were at the same age. They cannot attend the expensive residential and private schools that abound here, but must go to the government-aided schools with only basic facilities. Not many of their parents managed to go to school. They spent their lives working in the fields or delivering milk in the hill station. The lucky ones got into the army. Perhaps

Ranbir will do something different when he grows up.

He has yet to see a train but he sees planes flying over the mountains almost every day.

'How far can a plane go?' he asks.

'All over the world,' I tell him. 'Thousands of miles in a day. You can go almost anywhere.'

'I'll go round the world one day,' he vows. 'I'll buy a plane and go everywhere!'

And maybe he will. He has a determined chin and a defiant look in his eye.

The following lines in my journal were put down for my own inspiration or encouragement, but they will do for any determined young person:

> We get out of life what we bring to it. There is not a dream which may not come true if we have the energy which determines our own fate. We can always get what we want if we will it intensely enough... So few people succeed greatly because so few people conceive a great end, working towards it without giving up. We all know that the man who works steadily for money gets rich; the man who works day and night for fame or power reaches his goal. And those who work for deeper, more spiritual achievements will find them too. It may come when we no longer have any use for it, but if we have been willing it long enough, it will come!

◆

Up to a few years ago, very few girls in the hills or in the villages of India went to school. They helped in the home until they were old enough to be married, which wasn't very old. But there are now just as many girls as there are boys going to school.

Bindra is something of an extrovert—a confident fourteen-year-old who chatters away as she hurries down the road with her companions. Her father is a forest guard and knows me quite well; I meet him on my walks through the deodar woods behind Landour. And I had grown used to seeing Bindra almost every day. When she did not put in an appearance for a week, I asked her brother if anything was wrong.

'Oh, nothing,' he says, 'she is helping my mother cut grass. Soon the monsoon will end and the grass will dry up. So we cut it now and store it for the cows in winter.'

'And why aren't you cutting grass too?'

'Oh, I have a cricket match today,' he says, and hurries away to join his teammates. Unlike his sister, he puts pleasure before work!

Cricket, once the game of the elite, has become the game of the masses. On any holiday, in any part of this vast country, groups of boys can be seen making their way to the nearest field, or open patch of land, with bat, ball and any other cricketing gear that they can cobble together. Watching some of them play, I am amazed at the quality of talent, at the finesse with which they bat or bowl. Some of the local teams are as good, if not better, than any from the private schools, where there are better facilities. But the boys from these poor or lower middle-class families will never get the exposure that is necessary to bring them to the attention of those who select state or national teams. They will never get near enough to the men of influence and power. They must continue to play for the love of the game, or watch their more fortunate heroes' exploits on television.

♦

As winter approaches and the days grow shorter, those children who live far away must quicken their pace in order to get home before dark. Ranbir and his friends find that darkness has fallen before they are halfway home.

'What is the time, Uncle?' he asks, as he trudges up the steep road past Ivy Cottage.

One gets used to being called 'Uncle' by almost every boy or girl one meets. I wonder how the custom began. Perhaps it has its origins in the folk tale about the tiger who refrained from pouncing on you if you called him 'uncle'. Tigers don't eat their relatives! Or do they? The ploy may not work if the tiger happens to be a tigress. Would you call her 'Aunty' as she (or your teacher!) descends on you?

It's dark at six and by then, Ranbir likes to be out of the deodar forest and on the open road to the village. The moon and the stars and the village lights are sufficient, but not in the forest, where it is dark even during the day. And the silent flitting of bats and flying-foxes, and the eerie hoot of an owl, can be a little disconcerting for the hardiest of children. Once Ranbir and the other boys were chased by a bear.

When he told me about it, I said, 'Well, now we know you can run faster then a bear!'

'Yes, but you have to run downhill when chased by a bear.' He spoke as one having long experience of escaping from bears. 'They run much faster uphill!'

'I'll remember that,' I said, 'thanks for the advice.' And I don't suppose calling a bear 'Uncle' would help.

Usually, Ranbir has the company of other boys, and they sing most of the way, for loud singing by small boys will silence owls and frighten away the forest demons. One of them plays a flute, and flute music in the mountains is always enchanting.

◆

Not only in the hills, but all over India, children are constantly making their way to and from school, in conditions that range from dust storms in the Rajasthan desert to blizzards in Ladakh and Kashmir. In the larger towns and cities, there are school buses, but in remote rural areas getting to school can pose a problem.

Most children are more than equal to any obstacles that may arise. Like those youngsters in the Ganjam district of Orissa. In the absence of a bridge, they swim or wade across the Dhanei river everyday in order to reach their school. I have a picture of them in my scrapbook. Holding books or satchels aloft in one hand, they do the breaststroke or dog paddle with the other; or form a chain and help each other across.

Wherever you go in India, you will find children helping out with the family's source of livelihood, whether it be drying fish on the Malabar Coast, or gathering saffron buds in Kashmir, or grazing camels or cattle in a village in Rajasthan or Gujarat.

Only the more fortunate can afford to send their children to English-medium private or 'public' schools, and those children really are fortunate, for some of these institutions are excellent schools, as good, and often better, than their counterparts in Britain or USA. Whether it's in Ajmer or Bangalore, New Delhi or Chandigarh, Kanpur or Kolkata, the best schools set very high standards. The growth of a prosperous middle class has led to an ever-increasing demand for quality education. But as private schools proliferate, standards suffer too, and many parents must settle for the second-rate.

The great majority of our children still attend schools ran by the state or municipality. These vary from the good to the bad to the ugly, depending on how they are run and where they are situated. A classroom without windows, or with a roof that lets in the monsoon rain, is not uncommon. Even so, children from different communities learn to live and grow together. Hardship makes brothers of us all.

The census tells us that two in every five of the population is in the age group of five to fifteen. Almost half our population is on the way to school!

And here I stand at my window, watching some of them pass by—boys and girls, big and small, some scruffy, some smart, some mischievous, some serious, but all *going* somewhere—hopefully towards a better future.

OUR LOCAL TEAM

Here comes our batting hero;
Salutes the crowd, takes guard;
And out for zero.
He's in again
To strike a ton;
A lovely shot—
Then out for one.
Our demon bowler
Runs in quick;
He's really fast
Though hit for six.
In came their slogger:
He swung his bat
And missed by inches;
Our wicketkeeper's getting stitches.
Where's our captain?
In the deep.
What's he doing?
Fast asleep.

Last man in:
He kicks a boundary with his pad.
L.B.W.! Not out?
The ump's his dad!

SPELL BROKEN

We crouched before the singing fire
As the green wood writhed and bled
And the orange flames leapt higher
And your cheeks in the dark glowed red.
Alone in the forest, you and I; and then,
Came an old gypsy to warm his feet,
And shouting children, and two young men,
And pots and pans and a hunk of meat,
And a woman who shivered and sang to herself,
And a dog of enormous size!

You were laughing and singing an old love song,
Sweet as the whistling-thrush at dawn.
Swift as the running days of November,
Lost like a dream too brief to remember.

SIMPLY LIVING

These thoughts and observations were noted in my diaries through the 1980s, and may give readers some idea of the ups and downs, highs and lows, during a period when I was still trying to get established as an author.

March 1981

After a gap of twenty years, during which it was, to all practical purposes forgotten, *The Room on the Roof* (my first novel) gets reprinted in an edition for schools.

(This was significant, because it marked the beginning of my entry into the educational field. Gradually, over the years, more of my work became familiar to schoolchildren throughout the country.)

Stormy weather over Holi. Room flooded. Everyone taking turns with septic throats and fever. While in bed, read Stendhal's *Scarlet and Black*. I seem to do my serious reading only when I'm sick.

Felt well enough to take a leisurely walk down the Tehri Road. Trees in new leaf. The fresh light green of the maples is very soothing.

I may not have contributed anything towards the progress of civilization, but neither have I robbed the world of anything. Not one tree or bush or bird. Even the spider on my wall is welcome to his (her) space. Provided he (she) stays on the wall and does not descend on my pillow.

April

Swifts are busy nesting in the roof and performing acrobatics outside my window. They do everything on the wing, it seems—including feeding and making love. Mating in midair must be quite a feat.

Someone complimented me because I was 'always smiling'. I thought better of him for the observation and invited him over. Flattery will get you anywhere!

(This is followed by a three-month gap in my diary, explained by my next entry.)

Shortage of cash. Muddle, muddle, toil and trouble. I don't see myself—smiling.

Learn to zigzag. Try something different.

August

Kept up an article a day for over a month. Grub Street again!
DARE
WILL
KEEP SILENCE
These words helped Napoleon, but will they help me?
Try cursing!
I curse the block to money.
I curse the thing that takes all my effort away.
I curse all that would make me a slave.
I curse those who would harm my loved ones.

And now stop cursing and give thanks for all the good things you have enjoyed in life.

'We should not spoil what we have by desiring what we have not, but remember that what we have was the gift of fortune.' (Epicurus)

◆

'We ought to have more sense, of course, than to try to touch a dream, or to reach that place which exists but in the glamour of a name.'

(H.M. Tomlinson, *Tide Marks*)

October

A good year for the cosmos flower. Banks of them everywhere. They like the day-long sun. Clean and fresh—my favourite flower en masse.

But by itself, the wild commelina, sky-blue against dark green, always catches at the heart.

A latent childhood remains tucked away in our subconscious. This I have tried to explore...

A...stretches out on the bench like a cat, and the setting sun is trapped in his eyes, golden brown, glowing like tiger's eyes. (Oddly enough, this beautiful youth grew up to become a very sombre-looking padre.)

December

A kiss in the dark—warm and soft and all-encompassing—the moment stayed with me for a long time.

Wrote a poem, 'Who kissed me in the dark?' but it could not do justice to the kiss. Tore it up!

On the night of the 7th, light snowfall. The earliest that

I can remember it snowing in Landour. Early morning, the hillside looked very pretty, with a light mantle of snow covering trees, rusty roofs, vehicles at the bus stop—and concealing our garbage dump for a couple of hours, until it melted.

January 1982

Three days of wind, rain, sleet and snow. Flooded out of my bedroom. We convert dining room into dormitory. Everything is bearable except the wind, which cuts through these old houses like a knife—under the roof, through flimsy verandah enclosures and ill-fitting windows, bringing the icy rain with it.

Fed up with being stuck indoors. Walked up to Lal Tibba, in flurries of snow. Came back and wrote the story 'The Wind on Haunted Hill'.

I invoke Lakshmi, who shines like the full moon.
Her fame is all-pervading.
Her benevolent hands are like lotuses.
I take refuge in her lotus feet.
Let her destroy my poverty forever.
Goddess, I take shelter at your lotus feet.

February

My boyhood was difficult, but I had my dreams to sustain me. What does one dream about now?

But sometimes, when all else fails, a sense of humour comes to the rescue.

And the children (Raki, Muki, Dolly) bring me joy. All children do. Sometimes I think small children are the only sacred things left on this earth. Children and flowers.

Further blasts of wind and snow. In spite of the gloom, wrote a new essay.

March

Blizzard in the night. Over a foot of snow in the morning. And so it goes on...unprecedented for March. The Jupiter effect? At least the snow prevents the roof from blowing away, as happened last year. Facing east (from where the wind blows) doesn't help. And it's such a rickety old house.

◆

Mid-March and the first warm breath of approaching summer. Risk a haircut. Ramkumar does his best to make me look like a 1930s film star. I suppose I ought to try another barber, but he's too nice. 'I look rather strange,' I said afterwards (like Wallace Beery in *Billy the Kid*). 'Don't worry,' he said. 'You'll get used to it.'

'Why don't you give me an Amitabh Bachchan haircut?'

'You'll need more hair for that,' he says.

◆

Bus goes down the mud, killing several passengers. Death moves about at random, without discriminating between the innocent and the evil, the poor and the rich. The only difference is that the poor usually handle it better.

Late March

The blackest cloud I've ever seen squatted over Mussoorie, and then it hailed marbles for half an hour. Nothing like a hailstorm to clear the sky. Even as I write, I see a rainbow forming.

And Goddess Lakshmi smiles on me. An unprecedented flow of cheques, mainly accrued royalties on 'Angry River' and 'The Blue Umbrella'. A welcome change from last year's shortages and difficulties.

Perfection

The smallest insect in the world is a sort of fairy-fly and its body is only a fifth of a millimetre long. One can only just see it with the naked eye. Almost like a speck of dust, yet it has perfect little wings and little combs on its legs for preening itself.

Late April

Abominable cloud and chilly rain. But Usha brings bunches of wild roses and irises. And her own gentle smile.

Mid-May

Raki (after reading my biodata): 'Dada, you were born in 1934! And you are still here!' After a pause: 'You are very lucky.'

I guess I am, at that.

June

Did my sixth essay for *The Monitor* this year.

(Have written off and on, for *The Christian Science Monitor* of Boston from 1965 to 2002).

Wrote an article for a new magazine, *Keynote*, published in Bombay, and edited by Leela Naidu, Dom Moraes and David Davidar. It was to appear in the August issue. Now I'm told that the magazine has folded. (But David Davidar went on to bigger things with Penguin India!)

If at first you don't succeed, so much for skydiving.

July

Monsoon downpour. Bedroom wall crumbling. Landslide cuts off my walk down the Tehri road.

Usha: a complexion like apricot blossom seen through a mist.

September

Two dreams:

A constantly recurring dream or rather, nightmare—I am forced to stay longer than I had intended in a very expensive hotel and know that my funds are insufficient to meet the bill. Fortunately, I have always woken up before the bill is presented!

Possible interpretation: fear of insecurity. My own variation of the dream, common to many, of falling from a height but waking up before hitting the ground.

Another occasional dream: living in a house perched over a crumbling hillside. This one is not far removed from reality!

◆

Glorious day. Walked up and around the hill, and got some of the cobwebs out of my head.

That man is strongest who stands alone!

Some epigrams (for future use).

A well-balanced person: someone with a chip on both shoulders.

Experience: the knowledge that enables you to recognize a mistake when you make it the second time.

Sympathy: what one woman offers another in exchange for details.

Worry: the interest paid on trouble before it becomes due.

October

Some disappointment, as usual in connection with films (the screenplay I wrote for someone who wanted to remake *Kim*), but if I were to let disappointments get me down, I'd have given up writing twenty-five years ago.

A walk in the twilight. Soothing. Watched the winter-line

from the top of the hill.

Raki first in school races.

Savitri (Dolly) completes two years. Bless her fat little toes.

Advice to myself: conserve energy. Talk less!

'Better to have people wondering why you don't speak than to have them wondering why you speak.' (Disraeli)

♦

Wrote 'The Funeral'. One of my better stories, and thus more difficult to place.

If death was a thing that money could buy,

The rich they would live, and the poor they would die.

In California, you can have your body frozen after death in the hope that a hundred years from now some scientist will come along and bring you to life again. You pay in advance, of course.

December

I never have much luck with films or film-makers. Mr K.S. Varma finally (after five years) completed his film of my story 'The Last Tiger', but could not find a distributor for it. I don't regret the small sum I received for the story. He ran out of money—and tigers!—and apparently went to heroic lengths to complete the film in the forests of Bihar and Orissa. He used a circus tiger for the more intimate scenes, but this tiger disappeared one day, along with one of the actors. Tom Alter played a shikari and went on to play other, equally hazardous roles: he's still around, the tiger having spared him, but the film was never seen (and hasn't been seen to this day).

♦

A last postcard from an old friend:

> 'Ruskin, dear friend—but you won't be, unless you keep your word about lunching with us on Xmas Day. PLEASE DO COME, both Kanshi and I need your presence. It will be a small party this time as most of our friends are either *hors de combat* or dead! Bring Rakesh and Mukesh. Please let me know. I have been in bed for two days with a chill. Please don't disappoint.
>
> Love,
> Winnie'

(We did go to the Christmas party, but sadly, the chill became pneumonia and there were no more parties with Winnie and Kanshi, who were such good company. I still miss them.)

January 1984

To Maniram's home near Lal Tibba. He was brought up by his grandmother—his mother died when he was one. Keeps two calves, two cows (one brindled), and a pup of indeterminate breed. Made me swallow a glass of milk. Haven't touched milk for years, can't stand the stuff, but drank it so as not to hurt his feelings. (Mani and his Granny turned up in my children's story *Getting Granny's Glasses*.)

◆

On the 6th it was bitterly cold, and the snow came in through my bedroom roof. Not enough money to go away, but at least there's enough for wood and coal. I hate the cold—but the children seem to enjoy it. Raki, Muki and Dolly in constant high spirits.

◆

February

Two days and nights of blizzard—howling winds, hail, sleet, snow. Prem bravely goes out for coal and kerosene oil. Worst weather we've ever had up here. Sick of it.

♦

March

Peach, plum and apricot trees in blossom. Gentle weather at last. Schools reopen.

Sold German and Dutch translation rights in a couple of my children's books. I wish I could write something of lasting worth. I've done a few good stories but they are so easily lost in the mass of wordage that pours forth from the world's presses.

Here are some statistics which I got from the U.K. a couple of years ago:

There are over nine million books in the British Museum and they fill 86 miles of shelving.

There are over 50,000 living British authors. They don't get rich. The latest Society of Authors survey shows that only 55 per cent of those whose main occupation is writing earn over £700 a year.

Britain has 8,500 booksellers, as well as many other shops where books are sold.

The first book to be printed in Britain was *The Dictes and Sayings of the Philosophers,* which was translated and printed by William Caxton in 1477.

As many books were published in Britain between 1940 and 1980 as in the five centuries from Caxton's first book.

Who says the reading habit is dying?

♦

April

The 'adventure wind' of my boyhood—I felt it again today. Walked five miles to Suakholi, to look at an infinity of mountains.

The feeling of space—limitless space—can only be experienced by living in the mountains.

It is the emotional, the spiritual surge, that draws us back to the mountains again and again. It was not altogether a matter of mysticism or religion that prompted the ancients to believe that their gods dwelt in the high places of this earth. Those gods, by whatever name we know them, still dwell there. From time to time we would like to be near them, that we may know them and ourselves more intimately.

May

Completed my half century and launched into my 51st year.

Fifty is a dangerous age for most men. Last year there was nothing to celebrate, and at the end of it my diary went into the dustbin. There was an abortive and unhappy love affair (dear reader, don't fall in love at fifty!), a crisis in the home (with Prem missing for weeks), conflicts with publishers, friends, myself. So skip being fifty. Become fifty-one as soon its possible; you will find yourself in calmer waters. If you fall in love at the age of fifty, inner turmoil and disappointment is almost guaranteed. Don't listen to what the wise men say about love. P.G. Wodehouse said the whole thing more succinctly: 'You know, the way love can change a fellow is really frightful to contemplate.' Especially when a fifty-year-old starts behaving like a sixteen-year-old!

Most of my month's earnings went to the dentist. And I notice he's wearing a new suit.

June

A name—a lovely face—turn back the years: 45 years to be exact, when I was a small boy in Jamnagar, where my father taught English to some of the younger princes and princesses—among them M—whose picture I still have in my album (taken by my father). She wrote to me after reading something I'd written, wanting to know if I was the same little boy, i.e., Mr Bond's mischievous son. I responded, of course. A link with my father is so rare; and besides, I had a crush on her. My first love! So long ago—but it seems like yesterday...

◆

Monsoon breaks.
Money-drought breaks.
And if there's a connection, may the rain gods be generous this year.

(The rest of the year's entries were fairly mundane, implying that life at Ivy Cottage, Landour, went on pretty smoothly. But the rain gods played a trick or two. Although they were fairly generous to begin with, the year ended with a drought, as my mid-December entry indicates: 'Dust covers everything, after nearly two and half months of dry weather. Clouds build up, but disperse.' Always receptive to Nature's unpredictability, I wrote my story *Dust on the Mountain*.)

1995

On the flyleaf of this year's diary are written two maxims: 'Pull your own strings' and 'Act impeccably'. I'm not sure that I did either with much success, but I did at least try. And trying is what it's all about...

January

My book of poems and prayers finally published by Thomson Press, *seven years* after acceptance. Received a copy. Hope it won't be the only one. Splendid illustrations by Suddha. (Shortly afterwards Thomson Press closed down their children's book division and my book vanished too!)

Can thought (consciousness) exist outside the body? Can it be trained to do so? Can its existence continue after the body has gone? Does it *need* a body? (But without a body it would have nothing to do.)

Of course thoughts can travel. But do they travel of their own volition, or because of the bodily energy that sustains them?

We have the wonders of clairvoyance, of presentiments, and premonitions in dreams. How to account for these?

Our thinking is conditioned by past experience (including the past experience of the human race), and so, as Bergson said: 'We think with only a small part of the past, but it is with our entire past, including the original bent of the soul, that we desire, will, and act.'

'The original bent of the soul...' I accept that man has a soul, or he would be incapable of compassion.

February

We move from mind to matter:

Tried a pizza—seemed to take an hour to travel down my gullet.

Two days later: Swiss cheese pie with Mrs Goel who's Swiss—and more adventures of the digestive tract.

Next day: supper with the Deutschmanns from Australia. Australian pie.

Following day: rest and recovery. Then reverted to good

old dal bhaat.

Accompanied N—to Dehradun and ended up paying for our lunch. The trouble with rich people is that they never seem to have any money on them. That's how they stay rich, I suppose.

March

Sold *A Crow for All Seasons* to the Children's Film Society for a small sum. They think it will make a good animated film. And so it will. But I'm pretty sure they won't make it. They have forgotten about the story they bought from me five years ago! (Neither film was ever made.)

April

The wind in the pines and deodars hums and moans, but in the chestnut it rustles and chatters and makes cheerful conversation. The horse-chestnut in full leaf is a magnificent sight.

◆

Children down with mumps. I go down with a viral fever for two days. Recover and write three articles. Hope for the best. It is not in mortals to *command* success.

◆

Men get their sensual natures from their mothers, their intellectual makeup from their fathers; women, the other way round. (Or so I'm told!)

June

Not many years ago you had to walk for weeks to reach the pilgrim destinations—Badrinath, Gangotri, Kedarnath, Tungnath... Last week, within a few days, I covered them all, as most of them are now accessible by motorable road. I liked some of the smaller places, such as Nandprayag, which are still unspoilt. Otherwise, I'm afraid the dhaba-culture of urban India has followed the cars and buses into the mountains and up to the shrines.

July

The deodar (unlike the pine) is a hospitable tree. It allows other things to grow beneath it, and it tolerates growth upon its trunk and branches—moss, ferns, small plants. The tiny young cones are like blossoms on the dark green foliage at this time of the year.

♦

Slipped and cracked my head against the grid of a truck. Blood gushed forth, so I dashed across to Dr Joshi's little clinic and had three stitches and an anti-tetanus shot. Now you know why I don't travel well.

♦

M.C. Beautiful, seductive. 'She walks in beauty like the night...'

August

Endless rain. No sun for a week. But M.C. playful, loving. In good spirits, I wrote a funny story about cricket. I'd find it hard to write a serious story about cricket. The farcical element appeals to me more than the 'nobler' aspects of the game. Uncle Ken made more runs with his pads than with his bat. And out of every ten catches that came his way, he took one!

October

Paid rent in advance for next year; paid school fees to end of this year. Broke, but don't owe a paisa to a soul. Ice cream in town with Raki. Came home to find a couple of cheques waiting for me!

M.C. Quick as a vixen, but makes the chase worthwhile.
We walk in the wind and the rain. Exhilarating.
Frantic kisses.
Time to say goodbye!
When love is swiftly stolen,
It hasn't time to die.
When in love, I'm inspired to write bad verse.
Teilhard de Chardin said it better:
'Some day, after we have mastered the winds, the waves, the tides and gravity, we shall harness for God the energies of love. Then for the second time in the history of the world, man will have discovered fire.'

February 1986

Destiny is really the strength of our desires.

◆

Raki back from the village. I'm happy he has made himself popular there, adapted to both worlds, the comparative sophistication of Mussoorie and the simple earthiness of village Bachhanshu in the remoteness of Garhwal. Being able to get on with everyone, rich or poor, old or young, makes life so much easier. Or so I've found! My parents' broken marriage, father's early death, and the difficulties of adapting to my stepfather's home, resulted in my being something of a loner until I was thirty. Now I've become a family person without marrying. Selfish?

◆

Returned to two great comic novels—H. G. Wells's *History of Mr Polly* and George and Weedon Grossmith's *Diary of Nobody*. *Polly* has some marvellous set-pieces, while *Nobody* never fails to make me laugh.

◆

M. C. returns with a spring in the springtime. The same good nature and sense of humour.

> Three things in love the foolish will desire:
> Faith, constancy, and passion; but the wise
> Only an hour's happiness require
> And not to look into uncaring eyes.
>
> (Kenneth Hopkins)

March

Getting Granny's Glasses received a nomination for the Carnegie Medal. *Cricket for the Crocodile* makes friends.

After a cold wet spell, Holi brings warmer days, ladybirds, new friends.

May

So now I'm 52. Time to pare life down to the basics of doing.

a) what I have to do
b) what I want to do

Much prefer the latter.

June

Blood pressure up and down.

Writing for a living: It's a battlefield!

People do ask funny questions. Accosted on the road by a stranger, who proceeds to cross-examine me, starting with: 'Excuse me, are you a good writer?' For once, I'm stumped for an answer.

Muki no better. Bangs my study door, sees me give a start, and says, 'This door makes a lot of noise, doesn't it?'

August

Thousands converge on the town from outlying villages, for local festival. By late evening, scores of drunks staggering about on the road. A few fights, but largely good-natured.

The women dress very attractively and colourfully. But for most of the menfolk, the height of fashion appears to be a new pyjama-suit. But I'm a pyjama person myself. Pyjamas are comfortable, I write better wearing pyjamas!

September

Month began with a cheque that bounced. Refrained from checking my blood pressure.

◆

Monsoon growth at its peak. The ladies' slipper orchids are tailing off, but I noticed all the following wild flowers: balsam (two kinds), commelina, agrnnony, wild geranium (very pretty), sprays of white flowers emanating from the wild ginger, the scarlet fruit of the cobra lily just forming tiny mushrooms set like pearls in a retaining wall; ferns still green, which means more rain to come; escaped dahlias everywhere; wild begonias and much else. The best time of year for wild flowers.

February 1987

Home again, after five days in hospital with bleeding ulcers. Loving care from Prem. Support from Ganesh and others. Nurse Nirmala very caring. I prefer nurses to doctors.

Milk, hateful milk!

After a week, back in hospital. Must have been all that milk. Or maybe Nurse Nirmala!

March

To Delhi for a check-up. Public gardens ablaze with flowers. Felt much better.

'A merry heart does good like a medicine, but a broken spirit dries the bones.'

'He who tenderly brings up his servant from a child, shall have him become his son at the end.'

(Book of Proverbs)

May

Lines for future use:

Lunch (at my convent school) was boiled mutton and overcooked pumpkin, which made death lose some of its sting.

Pictures on the wall are not just something to look at. After a time, they become company.

Another bus accident, and a curious crowd gathered with disaster-inspired speed.

He (Upendra) has a bonfire of a laugh.

(Forgot to use these lines, so here they are!)

May

Ordered a birthday cake, but it failed to arrive. Sometimes I think inertia is the greatest force in the world.

Wrote a ghost story, something I enjoy doing from time to time, although I must admit that, try as I might, I have yet to encounter a supernatural being. Unless you can count dreams as being supernatural experiences.

August

After the drought, the deluge.

Landslide near the house. It rumbled away all night and I kept getting up to see how close it was getting to us. About twenty feet away. The house is none too stable, badly in need of repairs. In fact, it looks a bit like the Lucknow Residency after the rebels had finished shelling it.

(It did, however, survive the landslide, although the retaining wall above our flat collapsed, filling the sitting-room with rubble.)

November

To Delhi, to receive a generous award from Indian Council for Child Education. Presented to me by the vice president of India. Got back to my host's home to discover that the envelope contained another awardee's cheque. He was due to leave for Ahmedabad by train. Rushed to railway station, to find him on the platform studying my cheque which he had just discovered in his pocket. Exchanged cheques. All's well that ends well.

A Delhi Visit

A long day's taxi journey to Delhi. It gets tiring towards the end, but I have always found the road journey interesting and at times quite enchanting—especially the rural scene from outside Dehradun, through Roorkee and various small wayside towns, up to Muzzafarnagar and the outskirts of Meerut: the sugar cane being harvested and taken to the sugar factories (by cart or truck); the fruit on sale everywhere (right now, it's the season for bananas and 'chakotra' lemons); children bathing in small canals; the serenity of mango groves...

Of course there's the other side to all this—the litter that accumulates wherever there are large centres of population; the blaring of horns; loudspeakers here and there. It's all part of the picture. But the picture as a whole is a fascinating one, and the colours can't be matched anywhere else.

Marigolds blaze in the sun. Yes, whole fields of them, for they are much in demand on all sorts of ceremonial occasions: marriages, temple pujas, and garlands for dignitaries—making the humble marigold a good cash crop.

And not so humble after all. For although the rose may still be the queen of flowers, and the jasmine the princess of fragrance, the marigold holds its own through sheer sturdiness, colour and cheerfulness. It is a cheerful flower, no doubt about that—brightening up winter days, often when there is little else in bloom. It doesn't really have a fragrance—simply an acid odour, not to everyone's liking—but it has a wonderful range of colour, from lower yellow to deep orange to golden bronze, especially among the giant varieties in the hills.

Otherwise this is not a great month for flowers, although at the India International Centre (IIC) in Delhi, where I am staying, there is a pretty tree with fragile pink flowers—the Chorisnia speciosa, each bloom having five large pink petals, with long pistula.

BOY IN A BLUE PULLOVER

Boy in a faded blue pullover,
Poor boy, thin smiling boy,
Ran down the road shouting,
Singing, flinging his arms wide.
I stood in the way and stopped him.
'What's up?' I said. 'Why are you happy?'
He showed me the shining five rupee.
'I found it on the road,' he said.

And he held it to the light
That he might see it shining bright.

'And how will you spend it,
Small boy in a blue pullover?'
'I'll buy—I'll buy—
I'll buy a buckle for my belt,
Slim boy, smart boy,
Would buy a buckle for his belt...
Coin clutched in his hot hand,
He ran off laughing, bright.
The coin I'd lost an hour ago;
But better his that night.

GARHWAL HIMALAYA

Deep in the crouching mist lie the mountains.
Climbing the mountains are forests
Of rhododendron, spruce and deodar—
Trees of God, we call them—sighing
In the wind from the passes of Garhwal;
And the snow leopard moans softly
Where the herdsmen pass, their lean sheep cropping
Short winter grass.

And clinging to the sides of the mountains,
The small stone houses of Garhwal;
Then thin fields of calcinated soil torn
From the old spirit-haunted rocks;
Pale women plough, they laugh at the thunder,
And their men go down to the plains:
Little grows on the beautiful mountains
In the north wind.

There is hunger of children at noon; yet
There are those who sing of sunsets
And the gods and glories of Himachal,

Forgetting no one eats sunsets.
Wonder, then, at the absence of old men;
For some grow old at their mother's breasts,
In cold Garhwal.

A SONG OF MANY RIVERS

1

When I look down from the heights of Landour to the broad Valley of the Doon far below, I can see the little Suswa river, silver in the setting sun, meandering through fields and forests on its way to its confluence with the Ganga.

The Suswa is a river I knew well as a boy, but it has been many years since I took a dip in its quiet pools or rested in the shade of the tall spreading trees growing on its banks. Now I see it from my windows, far away, dreamlike in the mist, and I keep promising myself that I will visit it again, to touch its waters, cool and clear, and feel its rounded pebbles beneath my feet.

It's a little river, flowing down from the ancient Siwaliks and running the length of the valley until, with its sister river the Song, it slips into the Ganga just above the holy city of Haridwar. I could wade across (except during the monsoon when it was in spate) and the water seldom rose above the waist except in sheltered pools, where there were shoals of small fish.

There is a little known and charming legend about the Suswa and its origins, which I have always treasured. It tells us that the Hindu sage, Kasyapa, once gave a great feast to which all the gods were invited. Now Indra, the god of rain, while on his way to the entertainment, happened to meet 60,000 'balkhils' (pygmies) of the Brahmin caste, who were trying in vain to cross a cow's footprint filled with water—to them, a vast lake!

The god could not restrain his amusement. Peals of thunderous laughter echoed across the hills. The indignant Brahmins, determined to have their revenge, at once set to work creating a second Indra, who should supplant the reigning god. This could only be cloned by means of penance, fasting and self-denial, in which they persevered until the sweat flowing from their tiny bodies created the 'Suswa' or 'flowing waters' of the little river.

Indra, alarmed at the effect of these religious exercises, sought the help of Brahma, the creator, who taking on the role of a referee, interceded with the priests. Indra was able to keep his position as the rain god.

I saw no pygmies or fairies near the Suswa, but I did see many spotted deer, cheetal, coming down to the water's edge to drink. They are still plentiful in that area.

2
The Nautch Girl's Curse

At the other end of the Doon, far to the west, the Yamuna comes down from the mountains and forms the boundary between the states of Himachal and Uttaranchal. Today, there's a bridge across the river, but many years ago, when I first went across, it was by means of a small cable car, and a very rickety one at that.

During the monsoon, when the river was in spate, the only way across the swollen river was by means of this swaying trolley, which was suspended by a steel rope to two shaky wooden platforms on either bank. There followed a tedious bus journey, during which some sixty-odd miles were covered in six hours.

And then you were at Nahan, a small town a little over 3,000 feet above sea level, set amids hill slopes thick with sal and shishann trees. This charming old town links the subtropical Siwaliks to the first foothills of the Himalayas, a unique situation.

The road from Dagshai and Shimla nuns into Nahan from the north. No matter in which direction you look, the view is a fine one. To the south stretches the grand panorama of the plains of Saharanpur and Ambala, fronted by two low ranges of thickly forested hills. In the valley below, the pretty Markanda river winds its way out of the Kadir valley.

Nahan's main street is curved and narrow, but well-made and paved with good stone. To the left of the town is the former raja's palace. Nahan was once the capital of the state of Sirmur, now part of Himachal Pradesh. The original palace was built some three or four hundred years ago, but has been added to from time to time, and is now a large collection of buildings mostly in the Venetian style.

I suppose Nahan qualifies as a hill station, although it can be quite hot in summer. But unlike most hill stations, which are less than two hundred years old, Nahan is steeped in legend and history.

The old capital of Sirmur was destroyed by an earthquake some seven to eight hundred years ago. It was situated some twenty-four miles from present day Nahan, on the west bank of the Giri, where the river expands into a lake. The ancient capital was totally destroyed, with all its inhabitants, and apparently no record was left of its then ruling family. Little remained of the ancient city, just a ruined temple and a few broken stone figures.

As to the cause of the tragedy, the traditional story is that a nautch girl happened to visit Sirmur, and performed some wonderful feats. The Raja challenged the girl to walk safely over the Giri on a rope, offering her half his kingdom if she was successful.

The girl accepted the challenge. A rope was stretched across the river. But before starting out, the girl promised that if she fell victim to any treachery on the part of the raja, a curse would fall upon the city and it would be destroyed by a terrible catastrophe.

While she was on her way to successfully carrying out the feat, some of the raja's people cut the rope. She fell into the river and drowned. As predicted, total destruction came to the town.

The founder of the next line of the Sirmur Raja came from the Jaisalmer family in Rajasthan. He was on a pilgrimage to Haridwar with his wife when he heard of the catastrophe that had immolated every member of the state's ancient dynasty. He went at once with his wife into the territory, and established a Jaisalmer Raj. The descent from the first Rajput ruler of Jaisalmer stock, some seven hundred years ago, followed from father to son in an unbroken line. And after much intitial moving about, Nahan was fixed upon as the capital.

The territory was captured by the Gurkhas in 1803, but twelve years later they were expelled by the British after some severe fighting, to which a small English cemetery bears witness. The territory was restored to the raja, with the exception of the Jaunsar Bawar region.

Six or seven miles north of Nahan lies the mountain of Jaitak, where the Gurkhas made their last desperate stand. The place is worth a visit, not only for seeing the remains of the Gurkha Fort, but also for the magnificent view the mountain commands.

From the northernmost of the mountain's twin peaks, the whole south face of the Himalayas may be seen. From west to north you see the rugged prominences of the Jaunsar Bawar, flanked by the Mussoorie range of hills. It is wild mountain scenery, with a few patches of cultivation and little villages nestling on the sides of the hills. Garhwal and Dehradun are to the east, and as you go downhill you can see the broad sweep of the Yamuna as it cuts its way through the western Siwaliks.

3
Gently flows the Ganga

The Bhagirathi is a beautiful river, gentle and caressing (as compared to the turbulent Alaknanda), and pilgrims and others have responded to it with love and respect. The god Shiva released the waters of Goddess Ganga from his locks, and she sped towards the plains in the tracks of Prince Bhagirath's chariot.

> He held the river on his head
> And kept her wandering, where
> Dense as Himalaya's woods were spread
> The tangles of his hair.

Revered by Hindus and loved by all, Goddess Ganga weaves her spell over all who come to her. Some assert that the true Ganga (in its upper reaches) is the Alaknanda. Geographically, this may be so. But tradition carries greater weight in the abode of the Gods, and traditionally the Bhagirathi is the Ganga. Of course, the two rivers meet at Devprayag, in the foothills, and this marriage of the waters settles the issue.

I put the question to my friend Dr Sudhakar Misra, from whom words of wisdom sometimes flow; and true to form, he answered, 'The Alaknanda is Ganga, but the Bhagirathi is Ganga-ji.'

She issues from the very heart of the Himalayas. Visiting Gangotri in 1820, the writer and traveller Baillie Fraser noted, 'We are now in the centre of the Himalayas, the loftiest and perhaps the most rugged range of mountains in the world.'

Here, at the source of the river, we come to the realization that we are at the very centre and heart of things. One has an almost primaeval sense of belonging to these mountains and to this valley in particular. For me, and for many who have been here, the Bhagirathi is the most beautiful of the four main river valleys of Garhwal.

The Bhagirathi seems to have everything—a gentle disposition, deep glens and forests, the ultravision of an open valley graced with tiers of cultivation leading up by degrees to the peaks and glaciers at its head.

At Tehri, the big dam slows down Prince Bhagirath's chariot. But upstream, from Bhatwari to Harsil, there are extensive pine forests. They fill the ravines and plateaus, before giving way to yew and cypress, oak and chestnut. Above 9,000 feet the deodar (devdar, tree of the gods) is the principal tree. It grows to a little distance above Gangotri, and then gives way to the birch, which is found in patches to within half a mile of the glacier.

It was the valuable timber of the deodar that attracted the adventurer Frederick 'Pahari' Wilson to the valley in the 1850s. He leased the forests from the Raja of Tehri, and within a few years he had made a fortune. From his horse and depot at Harsil, he would float the logs downstream to Tehri, where they would be sawn up and despatched to buyers in the cities.

Bridge-building was another of Wilson's ventures. The most famous of these was a 350-feet suspension bridge at Bhaironghat, over 1,200 feet above the young Bhagirathi where it thunders through a deep defile. This rippling contraption was at first a source of terror to travellers, and only a few ventured across it.

To reassure people, Wilson would mount his horse and gallop to and fro across the bridge. It has since collapsed, but local people will tell you that the ghostly hoof beats of Wilson's horse can still be heard on full moon nights. The supports of the old bridge were massive deodar trunks, and they can still be seen to one side of the new road bridge built by engineers of the Northern Railway.

The old forest rest houses at Dharasu, Bhatwari and Harsil were all built by Wilson as staging posts, for the only roads were narrow tracks linking one village to another. Wilson married a local girl, Gulabi, from the village of Mukhba, and the portraits of the Wilsons (early examples of the photographer's art) still hang in these sturdy little bungalows. At any rate, I found their pictures at Bhatwari. Harsil is now out of bounds to civilians, and I believe part of the old house was destroyed in a fire a few years ago. This sturdy building withstood the earthquake which devastated the area in 1991.

Amongst other things, Wilson introduced the apple into this area, 'Wilson apples'—large, red and juicy—sold to travellers and pilgrims on their way to Gangotri. This fascinating man also acquired an encyclopaedic knowledge of the wildlife of the region, and his articles, which appeared in *Indian Sporting Life* in the 1860s, were later plundered by so-called wildlife writers for their own works.

He acquired properties in Dehradun and Mussoorie, and his wife lived there in some style, giving him three sons. Two died young. The third, Charlie Wilson, went through most of his father's fortune. His grave lies next to my grandfather's grave in the old Dehradun cemetery. Gulabi is buried in Mussoorie, next to her husband. I wrote this haiku for her:

Her beauty brought her fame,
But only the wild rose growing beside her grave
Is there to hear her whispered name—
Gulabi.

I remember old Mrs Wilson, Charlie's widow, when I was a boy in Dehra. She lived next door in what was the last of the Wilson properties. Her nephew, Geoffrey Davis, went to school with me in Shimla, and later joined the Indian Air Force. But luck never went the way of Wilson's descendants, and Geoffrey died when his plane crashed.

Wilson's life is fit subject for a romance; but even if one were never written, his legend would live on, as it has done for over a hundred years. There has never been any attempt to commemorate him, but people in the valley still speak of him in awe and admiration, as though he had lived only yesterday.

Some men leave a trail of legend behind them because they give their spirit to the place where they have lived, and remain forever a part of the rocks and mountain streams.

Gangotri is situated at just a little over 10,300 feet. On the right bank of the river is the Gangotri temple, a small neat building without too much ornamentation, built by Amar Singh Thapa, a Nepali General, early in the nineteenth century. It was renovated by the Maharaja of Jaipur in the 1920s. The rock on which it stands is called Bhagirath Shila and is said to be the place where Prince Bhagirath did penance in order that Ganga be brought down from her abode of eternal snow. Here the rocks are carved and polished by ice and water, so smooth that in places they look like rolls of silk. The fast flowing waters of this mountain torrent look very different from the huge sluggish river that finally empties its waters into the Bay of Bengal fifteen hundred miles away.

The river emerges from beneath a great glacier, thickly studded with enormous loose rocks and earth. The glacier is about a mile in width and extends upwards for many miles. The chasm in the glacier through which the stream rushed forth into the light of day is named Gaumukh, the cow's mouth, and is held in deepest reverence by Hindus. The regions of eternal frost in the vicinity were the scene of many of their most sacred mysteries.

The Ganga enters the world no puny stream, but bursts from its icy womb a river thirty or forty yards in breadth. At Gauri Kund (below the Gangotri temple) it falls over a rock of considerable height and continues tumbling over a succession of small cascades until it enters the Bhaironghati gorge.

A night spent beside the river, within the sound of the fall, is an eerie experience. After some time it begins to sound, not like one fall but a hundred, and this sound permeates both one's dreams and waking hours. Rising early to greet the dawn proved rather pointless at Gangotri, for the surrounding peaks did not let the sun in till after 9 a.m. Everyone rushed about to keep warm, exclaiming delightedly at what they call 'gulabi thand', literally, 'rosy cold'. Guaranteed to turn the cheeks a rosy pink! A charming expression, but I prefer a rosy sunburn, and remained beneath a heavy quilt until the sun came up to throw its golden shafts across the river.

This is mid-October, and after Diwali the shrine and the small township will close for winter, the pandits retreating to the relative warmth of Mukbha. Soon snow will cover everything, and even the hardy purple-plumaged whistling thrushes, lovers of deep shade, will move further down the valley. And down below the forest-line, the Garhwali farmers go about harvesting their terraced fields which form patterns of yellow, green and gold above the deep green of the river.

Yes, the Bhagirathi is a green river. Although deep and swift, it does not lose its serenity. At no place does it look hurried or confused—unlike the turbulent Alaknanda, fretting and frothing as it goes crashing down its boulder-strewn bed. The Alaknanda gives one a feeling of being trapped, because the river itself is trapped. The Bhagirathi is free-flowing, easy. At all times and places it seems to find its true level.

In the old days, only the staunchest of pilgrims visited the shrines at Gangotri and Jamnotri. The roads were rocky and dangerous, winding along in some places, ascending and descending the faces of deep precipices and ravines, at times leading along banks of loose earth where landslides had swept the original path away.

There are still no large towns above Uttarkashi, and this absence of large centres of population may be reason why the forests are better preserved than those in the Alaknanda valley, or further downstream. Uttarkashi, though a large and growing town, is as yet uncrowded. The seediness of towns like Rishikesh and parts of Dehradun is not yet evident here. One can take a leisurely walk through its long (and well-supplied) bazaar, without being jostled by crowds or knocked over by three-wheelers. Here, too, the river is always with you, and you must live in harmony with its sound as it goes rushing and humming along its shingly bed.

Uttarkashi is not without its own religious and historical importance, although all traces of its ancient town of Barahat appear to have vanished. There are four important temples here, and on the occasion of Makar Sankranti, early in January a week-long fair is held when thousands from the surrounding areas throng the roads to the town. To the beating of drums and blowing of trumpets, the gods and goddesses are brought to the fair in gaily decorated palanquins. The surrounding villages wear a deserted look that day as everyone flocks to the temples and bathing ghats and to the entertainments of the fair itself.

We have to move far downstream to reach another large centre of population, the town of Tehri, and this is a very different place from Uttarkashi. Tehri has all the characteristics of a small town in the plains—crowds, noise, traffic congestion, dust and refuse, scruffy dhabas—with this difference that here it is all ephemeral, for Tehri is destined to be submerged by the water of the Bhagirathi when the Tehri dam is finally completed.

The rulers of Garhwal were often changing their capitals, and when, after the Gurkha War (of 1811-15), the former capital of Srinagar became part of British Garhwal, Raja Sudershan Shah established his new capital at Tehri. It is said that when he reached this spot, his horse refused to go any further. This was enough for the king, it seems; or so the story goes.

Perhaps Prince Bhagirath's chariot will come to a halt here too, when the dam is built. The two hundred and forty-six metre high earthen dam, with forty-two square miles of reservoir capacity, will submerge the town and about thirty villages.

But as we leave the town and cross the narrow bridge over the river, a mighty blast from above sends rocks hurtling down the defile, just to remind us that work is indeed in progress.

Unlike the Raja's horse, I have no wish to be stopped in my tracks at Tehri. There are livelier places upstream. And as for Ganga herself, that deceptively gentle river, I wonder if she will take kindly to our efforts to contain her.

4
Falling for Mandakini

A great river at its confluence with another great river is, for me, a special moment in time. And so it was with the Mandakini at Rudraprayag, where its waters joined the waters of the Alaknanda, the one having come from the glacial snows above Kedarnath, the other from the Himalayan heights beyond Badrinath. Both sacred rivers, destined to become the holy Ganga further downstream.

I fell in love with the Mandakini at first sight. Or was it

the valley that I fell in love with? I am not sure, and it doesn't really matter. The valley is the river.

While the Alaknanda valley, especially in its higher reaches, is a deep and narrow gorge where precipitous outcrops of rock hang threateningly over the traveller, the Mandakini valley is broader, gentler, the terraced fields wider, the banks of the river a green sward in many places. Somehow, one does not feel that one is at the mercy of the Mandakini whereas one is always at the mercy of the Alaknanda with its sudden floods.

Rudraprayag is hot. It is probably a pleasant spot in winter, but at the end of June, it is decidedly hot. Perhaps its chief claim to fame is that it gave its name to the dreaded man-eating leopard of Rudraprayag, who in the course of seven years (1918-25) accounted for more than 300 victims. It was finally shot by Jim Corbett, who recounted the saga of his long hunt for the killer in his fine book, *The Man-eating Leopard of Rudraprayag*.

The place at which the leopard was shot was the village of Gulabrai, two miles south of Rudraprayag. Under a large mango tree stands a memorial raised to Jim Corbett by officers and Men of the Border Roads Organisation. It is a touching gesture to one who loved Garhwal and India. Unfortunately, several buffaloes are tethered close by, and one has to wade through slush and buffalo dung to get to the memorial stone. A board tacked on to the mango tree attracts the attention of motorists who might pass without noticing the memorial, which is off to one side.

The killer leopard was noted for its direct method of attack on humans; and, in spite of being poisoned, trapped in a cave, and shot at innumerable times, it did not lose its contempt for man. Two English sportsmen covering both ends to the old suspension bridge over the Alaknanda fired several times at the man-eater but to little effect.

It was not long before the leopard acquired a reputation among the hill folk for being an evil spirit. A sadhu was suspected of turning into the leopard by night, and was only saved from being lynched by the ingenuity of Philip Mason, then deputy commissioner of Garhwal. Mason kept the sadhu in custody until the leopard made his next attack, thus proving the man innocent. Years later, when Mason turned novelist and (using the pen name Philip Woodruffe) wrote *The Wild Sweet Witch*, he had one of the characters, a beautiful young woman who apparently turns into a man-eating leopard by night.

Corbett's host at Gulabrai was one of the few who survived an encounter with the leopard. It left him with a hole in his throat. Apart from being a superb story teller, Corbett displayed great compassion for people from all walks of life and is still a legend in Garhwal and Kumaon amongst people who have never read his books.

In June, one does not linger long in the steamy heat of Rudraprayag. But as one travels up the river, making a gradual ascent of the Mandakini valley, there is a cool breeze coming down from the snows, and the smell of rain is in the air.

The thriving little township of Agastmuni spreads itself along the wide river banks. Further upstream, near a little place called Chandrapuri, we cannot resist breaking our journey to sprawl on the tender green grass that slopes gently clown to the swift flowing river. A small rest house is in the making. Around it, banana fronds sway and poplar leaves dance in the breeze.

This is no sluggish river of the plains, but a fast moving current, tumbling over rocks, turning and twisting in its efforts to discover the easiest way for its frothy snow-fed waters to escape the mountains. Escape is the word! For the constant plaint of many a Garliwali is that, while his hills abound in rivers, the water runs down and away, and little if any reaches the fields and villages above it. Cultivation must depend on the rain and not on the river.

The road climbs gradually, still keeping to the river. Just outside Guptakashi, my attention is drawn to a clump of huge trees sheltering a small but ancient temple. We stop here and enter the shade of the trees.

The temple is deserted. It is a temple dedicated to Shiva, and in the courtyard are several river-rounded stone lingams on which leaves and blossoms have fallen. No one seems to come here, which is strange, since it is on the pilgrim route. Two boys from a neighbouring field leave their yoked bullock to come and talk to me, but they cannot tell me much about the temple except to confirm that it is seldom visited. 'The buses do not stop here.' That seems explanation enough. For where the buses go, the pilgrims go; and where the pilgrims go, other pilgrims will follow. Thus far and no further.

The trees seem to be magnolias. But I have never seen magnolia trees grow to such huge proportions. Perhaps they are something else. Never mind; let them remain a mystery.

Guptakashi in the evening is all a bustle. A coachload of pilgrims (headed for Kedarnath) has just arrived, and the tea shops near the bus-stand are doing brisk business. Then the 'local' bus from Ukhimath, across the river arrives, and many of the passengers head for a tea shop famed for its samosas. The local bus is called the *Bhook Hartal*, the 'Hunger-strike' bus.

'How did it get that name?' I asked one of the samosa-eaters.

'Well, it's an interesting story. For a long time we had been asking the authorities to provide a bus service for the local people and for the villagers who live off the roads. All the buses came from Srinagar or Rishikesh, and were taken up by pilgrims. The locals couldn't find room in them. But our pleas went unheard until the whole town, or most of it, decided to go on hunger-strike.'

'They nearly put me out of business too,' said the tea shop owner cheerfully. 'Nobody ate any samosas for two days!'

There is no cinema or public place of entertainment at Guptakashi, and the town goes to sleep early. And wakes early.

At six, the hillside, green from recent rain, sparkles in the morning sunshine. Snowcapped Chaukhamba (7,140 metres) is dazzling. The air is clear; no smoke or dust up here. The climate, I am told, is mild all the year round judging by the scent and shape of the flowers, and the boys call them Champs, Hindi for champa blossom. Ukhimath, on the other side of the river, lies in the shadow. It gets the sun at nine. In winter, it must wait till afternoon.

Guptakashi has not yet been rendered ugly by the barrack-type architecture that has come up in some growing hill towns. The old double storeyed houses are built of stone, with gray slate roofs. They blend well with the hillside. Cobbled paths meander through the old bazaar.

One of these takes up to the famed Guptakashi temple, tucked away above the old part of the town. Here, as in Benaras, Shiva is worshipped as Vishwanath, and two underground streams representing the sacred Jamuna and Bhagirathi rivers feed the pool sacred to the God. This temple gives the town its name, Gupta-Kashi, the 'Invisible Benaras', just as Uttarkashi on the Bhagirathi is 'Upper Benaras'.

Guptakashi and its environs have so many lingams that the saying *'June Kanhar Utne Shanhar'*—'As many stones, so many Shivas'—has become a proverb to describe its holiness.

From Guptakashi, pilgrims proceed north to Kedarnath, and the last stage of their journey—about a day's march—must be covered on foot or horseback. The temple of Kedarnath, situated at a height of 11,753 feet, is encircled by snowcapped peaks, and Atkinson has conjectured that 'the symbol of the linga may have arisen front the pointed peaks around his (God Shiva's) original home.'

The temple is dedicated to Sadashiva, the subterranean form of the God, who, 'fleeing from the Pandavas took refuge here in the form of a he-buffalo and finding himself hard- pressed, dived into the ground leaving the hinder parts on the surface, which continue to be the subject of adoration.' (Atkinson).

The other portions of the God are worshipped as follows: the arms at Tunguath, at a height of 13,000 feet, the face at Rudranath (12,000 feet), the belly at Madmaheshwar, 18 miles northeast of Guptakashi; and the hair and head at Kalpeshwar, near Joshimath. These five sacred shrines form the *Punch Kedar* (five Kedars).

We leave the Mandakini to visit Tungnath on the Chandrashila range. But I will return to this river. It has captured my mind and heart.

ADVENTURES IN READING

1
BEAUTY IN SMALL BOOKS

You don't see them so often now, those tiny books and almanacs—genuine pocket books—once so popular with our parents and grandparents; much smaller than the average paperback, often smaller than the palm of the hand. With the advent of coffee-table books, new books keep growing bigger and bigger, rivalling tombstones! And one day, like Alice after drinking from the wrong bottle, they will reach the ceiling and won't have anywhere else to go. The average publisher, who apparently believes that large profits are linked to large books, must look upon these old miniatures with amusement or scorn. They were not meant for a coffee table, true. They were meant for true book-lovers and readers, for they took up very little space—you could slip them into your pocket without any discomfort, either to you or to the pocket.

I have a small collection of these little books, treasured over the years. Foremost is my father's prayer-book and psalter, with his name, 'Aubrey Bond, Lovedale, 1917', inscribed on the inside back cover. Lovedale is a school in the Nilgiri Hills in south India, where, as a young man, he did his teacher's training. He gave it to me soon after I went to a boarding school in Shimla in 1944, and my own name is inscribed on it in his beautiful handwriting.

Another beautiful little prayer-book in my collection is called *The Finger Prayer Book*. Bound in soft leather, it is about the same length and breadth as the average middle finger. Replete with psalms, it is the complete book of common prayer and not an abridgement; a marvel of miniature book production.

Not much larger is a delicate item in calf-leather, *The Humour of Charles Lamb*. It fits into my wallet and often stays there. It has a tiny portrait of the great essayist, followed by some thirty to forty extracts from his essays, such as this favourite of mine: 'Every dead man must take upon himself to be lecturing me with his odious truism, that "Such as he is now, I must shortly be". Not so shortly friend, perhaps as thou imaginest. In the meantime, I am alive. I move about. I am worth twenty of thee. Know thy betters!'

No fatalist, Lamb. He made no compromise with Father Time. He affirmed that in age we must be as glowing and tempestuous as in youth! And yet Lamb is thought to be an old-fashioned writer.

Another favourite among my 'little' books is *The Pocket Trivet, An Anthology for Optimists*, published by *The Morning Post* newspaper in 1932. 'But what is a trivet?' the unenlightened may well ask. Well, it's a stand for a small pot or kettle, fixed securely over a grate. To be 'right as a trivet' is to be perfectly right. Just right, like the short sayings in this book, which is further enlivened by a number of charming woodcuts based on the seventeenth-century originals; such as the illustration of a moth hovering over a candle flame and below it the legend—'I seeke mine owne hurt.'

But the sayings are mostly of a cheering nature, such as Emerson's 'Hitch your wagon to a star!' or the West Indian proverb: 'Every day no Christmas, an' every day no rainy day.'

My book of trivets is a happy example of much concentrated wisdom being collected in a small space—the beauty separated from the dross. It helps me to forget the dilapidated building in which I live and to look instead, at the ever-changing cloud patterns as seen from my bedroom windows. There is no end to the shapes made by the clouds, or to the stories they set off in my head. We don't have to circle the world in order to find beauty and fulfilment. After all, most of living has to happen in the mind. And, to quote one anonymous sage from my trivet, 'The world is only the size of each man's head.'

2
WRITTEN BY HAND

Amongst the current fraternity of writers, I must be that very rare person—an author who actually writes by hand!

Soon after the invention of the typewriter, most editors and publishers understandably refused to look at any mansucript that was handwritten. A decade or two earlier, when Dickens and Balzac had submitted their hefty manuscripts in longhand, no one had raised any objection. Had their handwriting been awful, their manuscripts would still have been read. Fortunately for all concerned, most writers, famous or obscure, took pains over their handwriting. For some, it was an art in itself, and many of those early manuscripts are a pleasure to look at and read.

And it wasn't only authors who wrote with an elegant hand. Parents and grandparents of most of us had distinctive styles of their own. I still have my father's last letter, written to me when I was at boarding school in Shimla some fifty years ago. He used large, beautifully formed letters, and his thoughts seemed to have the same flow and clarity as his handwriting.

In his letter he advises me (then a nine-year-old) about my own handwriting; 'I wanted to write before about your writing. Ruskin.... Sometimes I get letters from you in very small writing, as if you wanted to squeeze everything into one sheet of letter paper. It is not good for you or for your eyes, to get into the habit of writing too small... Try and form a larger style of handwriting—use more paper if necessary!'

I did my best to follow his advice, and I'm glad to report that after nearly forty years of the writing life, most people can still read my handwriting!

Word processors are all the rage now, and I have no objection to these mechanical aids any more than I have to my old Olympia typewriter, made in 1956 and still going strong. Although I do all my writing in longhand, I follow the conventions by typing a second draft. But I would not enjoy my writing if I had to do it straight on to a machine. It isn't just the pleasure of writing longhand. I like taking my notebooks and writing-pads to odd places. This particular essay is being written on the steps of my small cottage facing Pari Tibba (Fairy Hill). Part of the reason for sitting here is that there is a new postman on this route, and I don't want him to miss me.

For a freelance writer, the postman is almost as important as a publisher. I could, of course, sit here doing nothing, but as I have pencil and paper with me, and feel like using them, I shall write until the postman comes and maybe after he has gone, too! There is really no way in which I could set up a word-processor on these steps.

There are a number of favourite places where I do my writing. One is under the chestnut tree on the slope above the cottage. Word processors were not designed keeping mountain slopes in mind. But armed with a pen (or pencil) and paper, I can lie on the grass and write for hours. On one occasion, last month, I did take my typewriter into the garden, and I am still trying to extricate an acorn from under the keys, while the roller seems permanently stained yellow with some fine pollen-dust from the deodar trees.

My friends keep telling me about all the wonderful things I can do with a word processor, but they haven't got around to finding me one that I can take to bed, for that is another place where I do much of my writing—especially on cold winter nights, when it is impossible to keep the cottage warm.

While the wind howls outside, and snow piles up on the windowsill, I am warm under my quilt, writing pad on my knees, ballpoint pen at the ready. And if, next day, the weather is warm and sunny, these simple aids will accompany me on a long walk, ready for instant use should I wish to record an incident, a prospect, a conversation, or simply a train of thought.

When I think of the great eighteenth and nineteenth century writers, scratching away with their quill pens, filling hundreds of pages every month, I am amazed to find that their handwriting did not deteriorate into the sort of hieroglyphics that often make up the average doctor's prescription today. They knew they had to write legibly, if only for the sake of the typesetters.

Both Dickens and Thackeray had good, clear, flourishing styles. (Thackeray was a clever illustrator, too.) Somerset Maugham had an upright, legible hand. Churchill's neat handwriting never wavered, even when he was under stress. I like the bold, clear, straightforward hand of Abraham Lincoln; it mirrors the man. Mahatma Gandhi, another great soul who fell to the assassin's bullet, had many similarities of both handwriting and outlook.

Not everyone had a beautiful hand. King Henry VIII had an untidy scrawl, but then, he was not a man of much refinement. Guy Fawkes, who tried to blow up the British Parliament, had a very shaky hand. With such a quiver, no wonder he failed in his attempt! Hitler's signature is ugly, as you would expect. And Napoleon's doesn't seem to know where to stop; how much like the man!

I think my father was right when he said handwriting was often the key to a man's character, and that large well-formed letters went with an uncluttered mind. Florence Nightingale had a lovely handwriting, the hand of a caring person. And there were many like her, amongst our forebears.

3
WORDS AND PICTURES

When I was a small boy, no Christmas was really complete unless my Christmas stocking contained several recent issues of my favourite comic paper. If today my friends complain that I am too voracious a reader of books, they have only these comics to blame; for they were the origin, if not of my tastes in reading, then certainly of the reading habit itself.

I like to think that my conversion to comics began at the age of five, with a comic strip on the children's page of *The Statesman*. In the late 1930s, Benji, whose head later appeared only on the Benji League badge, had a strip to himself; I don't remember his adventures very clearly, but every day (or was it once a week?) I would cut out the Benji strip and paste it into a scrapbook. Two years later this scrapbook, bursting with the adventures of Benji, accompanied me to boarding school, where, of course, it passed through several hands before finally passing into limbo.

Of course comics did not form the only reading matter that found its way into my Christmas stocking. Before I was eight, I had read *Peter Pan*, *Alice*, and most of *Mr Midshipman Easy*; but I had also consumed thousands of comic-papers which were, after all, slim affairs and mostly pictorial, 'certain little penny books radiant with gold and rich with bad pictures', as Leigh Hunt described the children's papers of his own time.

But though they were mostly pictorial, comics in those days did have a fair amount of reading matter, too. *The Hostspur, Wizard, Magnet* (a victim of the Second World War) and *Champion* contained stories woven round certain popular characters. In *Champion*, which I read regularly right through my prep school years, there was Rockfist Rogan, Royal Air Force (R.A.F.), a pugilist who managed to combine boxing with bombing, and Fireworks Flynn, a footballer who always scored the winning-goal in the last two minutes of play

Billy Bunter has, of course, become one of the immortals—almost a subject for literary and social historians. Quite recently, *The Times Literary Supplement* devoted its first two pages to an analysis of the Bunter stories. Eminent lawyers and doctors still look back nostalgically to the arrival of the weekly *Magnet*; they are now the principal customers for the special souvenir edition of the first issue of the *Magnet*, recently reprinted in facsimile. Bunter, 'forever young', has become a folk-hero. He is seen on stage, screen and television, and is even quoted in the House of Commons.

From this, I take courage. My only regret is that I did not preserve my own early comics—not because of any bibliophilic value which they might possess today, but because of my sentimental regard for early influences in art and literature.

The first venture in children's publishing, in 1774 was a comic of sorts. In that year, John Newberry brought out:

> According to Act of Parliament (neatly bound and gilt):
> A Little Pretty Pocket-Book, intended for the Instruction
> and Amusement of Little Master Tommy and Pretty Miss

> Polly, with an agreeable Letter to read from Jack the Giant-Killer...

The book contained pictures, rhymes and games. Newberry's characters and imaginary authors included Woglog the Giant, Tommy Trip, Giles Gingerbread, Nurse Truelove, Peregrine Puzzlebrains, Primrose Prettyface, and many others with names similar to those found in the comic-papers of our own century.

Newberry was also the originator of the 'Amazing Free Offer', so much a part of American comics. At the beginning of 1755, he had this to offer:

> Nurse Truelove's New Year gift, or the Book of Books for children, adorned with Cuts and designed as a present for every little boy who would become a great man and ride upon a fine horse; and to every little girl who would become a great woman and ride in a Lord Mayor's gilt coach. Printed for the author, who has ordered these books to be given gratis to all little boys in St Paul's churchyard, they paying for the binding, which is only two pence each book.

Many of today's comics are crude and, like many television serials violent in their appeal. But I did not know American comics until I was twelve, and by then I had become quite discriminating. Superman, Bulletman, Batman, and Green Lantern, and other super heroes all left me cold. I had, by then, passed into the world of real books but the weakness for the comic-strip remains. I no longer receive comics in my Christmas stocking; but I do place a few in the stockings of Gautam and Siddharth. And, needless to say, I read them right through beforehand.

MY FAR PAVILIONS

> Bright red
> The poinsettia flames,
> As autumn and the old year wanes.

When I have time on my hands, I write haikus, like the one above. This one brings back memories and images of my maternal grandmother's home in Dehradun, in the early 1940s. I say grandmother's home because, although grandfather built the house, he had passed on while I was still a child and I have no memories of him that I can conjure up. But he was someone about whom everyone spoke, and I learnt that he had personally supervised the building of the house, partially designing it on the lines of a typical Indian Railways bungalow—neat, compact, and without any frills. None of those Doric pillars, Gothic arches, and mediaeval turrets that characterized some of the Raj house for an earlier period. But instead of the customary red bricks, he used the smooth rounded stones from a local river bed, and this gave the bungalow a distinctive look.

In all the sixty-five years that I have lived in India, my grandparents' abode was the only house that gave me a feeling of some permanence, as neither my parents nor I were ever to own property. But India was my home, and it was big enough.

Grandfather looked after the mango and lichi orchard at the back of the house, grandmother looked after the flower garden in front. English flowers predominated—philox, larkspur, petunias, sweet peas, snapdragons, nasturtiums; but there was also a jasmine bush, poinsettias, and of course, lots of colourful bougainvillaea climbing the walls. And there were roses brought over from nearby Saharanpur. Saharanpur had become a busy railway junction and an industrial town, but its roses were still famous. It was the home of the botanical survey in northern India, and in the previous century many famous botanists and explorers had ventured into the Himalayas using Saharanpur as their base.

Grandfather had retired from the Railways and settled in Dehra around 1905. At this period, the small foothills town was becoming quite popular as a retreat for retiring Anglo-Indian and domiciled Europeans. The bungalows had large compounds and gardens, and Dehra was to remain a garden town until a few years after Independence. The Forest Research Institute, the Survey of India, the Indian Military Academy, and a number of good schools, made the town a special sort of place. By the mid fifties, the pressures of population meant a greater demand for housing, and gradually the large compounds gave way to housing estates, and the gardens and orchards began to disappear. Most of the estates were now owned by the prospering Indian middle classes. Some of them strove to maintain the town's character and unique charm—flower shows, dog shows, school fetes, club life, dances, garden parties—but gradually these diminished; and today, as the capital of the new state of Uttaranchal, Dehra is as busy, congested and glamorous as any northern town or New Delhi suburb.

My father was always on the move. As a young man, he had been a schoolteacher at Lovedale, in the Nilgiris, then an assistant manager on a tea estate in Travancore-Cochin (now Kerala). He had also worked in the Ichhapore Rifle Factory bordering Calcutta. At the time I was born, he was employed in the Kathiawar states, setting up little schools for the state children in Jamnagar, Pithadia and Jetpur. I grew up in a variety of dwellings, ranging from leaky old dak bungalows to spacious palace guesthouses. Then, during the Second World War, when he enlisted and was posted in Delhi, we moved from tent to Air Force hutment, to a flat in Scindia House, to rented rooms on Halley Road, Atul Grove, and elsewhere! When he was posted to Karachi, and then Calcutta, I was sent to boarding school in Shimla.

Father had, in fact, grown up in Calcutta, and his mother still lived at 14, Park Lane. She outlived all her children and continued to live at Park Lane until she was almost ninety. Last year, when I visited Calcutta, I found the Park Lane house. But it was boarded up. Nobody seemed to live there any more. Garbage was piled up near the entrance. A billboard hid most of the house from the road.

Possibly my boarding school, Bishop Cotton's in Shimla, provided me with a certain feeling of permanence, especially after I lost my father in 1944. Known as the 'Eton of the East', and run on English public school lines, Bishop Cotton's did not cater to individual privacy. Everyone knew what you kept in your locker. But when I became a senior, I was fortunate enough to be put in charge of the school library. I could use it in my free time, and it became my retreat, where I could read or write or just be on my own. No one bothered me there, for even in those pre-TV and pre-computer days there was no great demand for books! Reading was a minority pastime then, as it is now.

After school, when I was trying to write and sell my early short stories, I found myself ensconced in a tiny barsati, a room on the roof of an old lodging house in Dehradun. Alas! Granny's house had been sold by her eldest daugher, who had gone 'home' to England; my stepfather's home was full of half-brothers, stepbrothers and sundry relatives. The barsati gave me privacy.

A bed, a table and a chair were all that the room contained. It was all I needed. Even today, almost fifty years later, my room has the same basic furnishings, except that the table is larger, the bed is slightly more comfortable, and there is a rug on the floor, designed to trip me up whenever I sally forth from the room.

Then, as now, the view from the room, or from its windows, has always been an important factor in my life. I don't think I could stay anywhere for long unless I had a window from which to gaze out upon the world.

Dehradun isn't very far from where I live today, and I have passed granny's old bungalow quite often. It is really half a house now, a wall having been built through the centre of the compound. Like the country itself, it found itself partitioned, and there are two owners; one has the lichi trees and the other the mangoes. Good luck to both!

I do not venture in at the gate, I shall keep my memories intact. The only reminders of the past are a couple of potted geraniums on the verandah steps. And I shall sign off with another little haiku:

> Red geranium
> Gleaming against the rain-bright floor...
> Memory, hold the door!

JOYFULLY I WRITE

I am a fortunate person. For over fifty years I have been able to make a living by doing what I enjoy most—writing.

Sometimes I wonder if I have written too much. One gets into the habit of serving up the same ideas over and over again; with a different sauce perhaps, but still the same ideas, themes, memories, characters. Writers are often chided for repeating themselves. Artists and musicians are given more latitude. No one criticized Turner for painting so many sunsets at sea, or Gauguin for giving us all those lovely Tahitian women; or Husain for treating us to so many horses, or Jamini Roy for giving us so many identical stylized figures.

In the world of music, one Puccini opera is very like another, a Chopin nocturne will return to familiar themes, and in the realm of lighter, modern music the same melodies recur with only slight variations. But authors are often taken to task for repeating themselves. They cannot help this, for in their writing they are expressing their personalities. Hemingway's world is very different from Jane Austen's. They are both unique worlds, but they do not change or mutate in the minds of their author-creators. Jane Austen spent all her life in one small place, and portrayed the people she knew. Hemingway roamed the world, but his characters remained much the same, usually extensions of himself.

In the course of a long writing career, it is inevitable that a writer will occasionally repeat himself, or return to themes that have remained with him even as new ideas and formulations enter his mind. The important thing is to keep writing, observing, listening and paying attention to the beauty of words and their arrangement. And like artists and musicians, the more we work on our art, the better it will be.

Writing, for me, is the simplest and greatest pleasure in the world. Putting a mood or an idea into words is an occupation I truly love. I plan my day so that there is time in it for writing a poem, or a paragraph, or an essay, or part of a story or longer work; not just because writing is my profession, but from a feeling of delight.

The world around me—be it the mountains or the busy street below my window—is teeming with subjects, sights, thoughts, that I wish to put into words in order to catch the fleeting moment, the passing image, the laughter, the joy, and sometimes the sorrow. Life would be intolerable if I did not have this freedom to write every day. Not that everything I put down is worth preserving. A great many pages of manuscripts have found their way into my waste-paper basket or into the stove that warms the family room on cold winter evenings. I do not always please myself. I cannot always please others because, unlike the hard professionals, the Forsyths and the Sheldons, I am not writing to please everyone, I am really writing to please myself!

My theory of writing is that the conception should be as clear as possible, and that words should flow like a stream of clear water, preferably a mountain stream! You will, of course, encounter boulders, but you will learn to go over them or around them, so that your flow is unimpeded. If your stream gets too sluggish or muddy, it is better to put aside that particular piece of writing. Go to the source, go to the spring, where the water is purest, your thoughts as clear as the mountain air.

I do not write for more than an hour or two in the course of the day. Too long at the desk, and words lose their freshness.

Together with clarity and a good vocabulary, there must come a certain elevation of mood. Sterne must have been bubbling over with high spirits when he wrote *Shandy*. The sombre intensity of *Wuthering Heights* reflects Emily Bronte's passion for life, fully knowing that it was to be brief. Tagore's melancholy comes through in his poetry. Dickens is always passionate; there are no half measures in his work. Conrad's prose takes on the moods of the sea he knew and loved.

A real physical emotion accompanies the process of writing, and great writers are those who can channel this emotion into the creation of their best work.

'Are you a serious writer?' a schoolboy once asked.

'Well, I try to be *serious*,' I said, 'but cheerfulness keeps breaking in!'

Can a cheerful writer be taken seriously? I don't know. But I was certainly serious about making writing the main occupation of my life.

In order to do this, one has to give up many things—a job, security, comfort, domesticity—or rather, the pursuit of these things. Had I married when I was twenty-five, I would not have been able to throw up a good job as easily as I did at the time; I might now be living on a pension! God forbid. I am grateful for continued independence and the necessity to keep writing for my living, and for those who share their lives with me and whose joys and sorrows are mine too. An artist must not lose his hold on life. We do that when we settle for the safety of a comfortable old age.

Normally writers do not talk much, because they are saving their conversation for the readers of their books—those invisible listeners with whom we wish to strike a sympathetic chord. Of course, we talk freely with our friends, but we are reserved with people we do not know very well. If I talk too freely about a story I am going to write, chances are it will never be written. I have talked it to death.

Being alone is vital for any creative writer. I do not mean that you must live the life of a recluse. People who do not know me are frequently under the impression that I live in lonely splendour on a mountain top, whereas in reality, I share a small flat with a family of twelve—and I'm the twelfth man, occasionally bringing out refreshments for the players!

I love my extended family, every single individual in it, but as a writer I must sometimes get a little time to be alone with my own thoughts, reflect a little, talk to myself, laugh about all the blunders I have committed in the past, and ponder over the future. This is contemplation, not meditation. I am not very good at meditation, as it involves remaining in a passive state for some time. I would rather be out walking, observing the natural world, or sitting under a tree contemplating my novel or navel! I suppose the latter is a form of meditation.

When I casually told a journalist that I planned to write a book consisting of my meditations, he reported that I was writing a book on meditation per se, which gave it a different connotation. I shall go along with the simple dictionary meaning of the verb *meditate*—to plan mentally, to exercise the mind in contemplation.

So I was doing it all along!

◆

I am not, by nature, a gregarious person. Although I love people, and have often made friends with complete strangers, I am also a lover of solitude. Naturally, one thinks better when one is alone. But I prefer walking alone to walking with others. That ladybird on the wild rose would escape my attention if I was engaged in a lively conversation with a companion. Not that the ladybird is going to change my life. But by acknowledging its presence, stopping to admire its beauty, I have paid obeisance to the natural scheme of things of which I am only a small part.

It is upon a person's power of holding fast to such undimmed beauty that his or her inner hopefulness depends. As we journey through the world, we must inevitably encounter meanness and selfishness. As we fight for our survival, the higher visions and ideals often fade. It is then that we need ladybirds! Contemplating that tiny creature, or the flower on which it rests, gives one the hope—better, the certainty—that there is more to life than interest rates, dividends, market forces and infinite technology.

As a writer, I have known hope and despair, success and failure; some recognition but also long periods of neglect and critical dismissal. But I have had no regrets. I have enjoyed the writer's life to the full, and one reason for this is that living in India has given me certain freedoms which I would not have enjoyed elsewhere. Friendship when needed. Solitude when desired. Even, at times, love and passion. It has tolerated me for what I am—a bit of a dropout, unconventional, idiosyncratic. I have been left alone to do my own thing. In India, people do not censure you unless you start making a nuisance of yourself. Society has its norms and its orthodoxies, and provided you do not flaunt all the rules, society will allow you to go your own way. I am free to become a naked ascetic and roam the streets with a begging bowl; I am also free to live in a palatial farmhouse if I have the wherewithal. For twenty-five years, I have lived in this small, sunny second-floor room looking out on the mountains, and no one has bothered me, unless you count the neighbour's dog who prevents the postman and courier boys from coming up the steps.

◆

I may write for myself, but as I also write to get published, it must follow that I write for others too. Only a handful of readers might enjoy my writing, but they are my soulmates, my alter egos, and they keep me going through those lean times and discouraging moments.

Even though I depend upon my writing for a livelihood, it is still, for me, the most delightful thing in the world.

I did not set out to make a fortune from writing; I knew I was not that kind of writer. But it was the thing I did best, and I persevered with the exercise of my gift, cultivating the more discriminating editors, publishers and readers, never really expecting huge rewards but accepting whatever came my way. Happiness is a matter of temperament rather than circumstance, and I have always considered myself fortunate in having escaped the tedium of a nine-to-five job or some other form of drudgery.

Of course, there comes a time when almost every author asks himself what his effort and output really amounts to. We expect our work to influence people, to affect a great many readers, when in fact, its impact is infinitesimal. Those who work on a large scale must feel discouraged by the world's indifference. That is why I am happy to give a little innocent pleasure to a handful of readers. This is a reward worth having.

As a writer, I have difficulty in doing justice to momentous events, the wars of nations, the politics of power; I am more at ease with the dew of the morning, the sensuous delights of the day, the silent blessings of the night, the joys and sorrows of children, the strivings of ordinary folk and, of course, the ridiculous situations in which we sometimes find ourselves.

We cannot prevent sorrow and pain and tragedy. And yet when we look around us, we find that the majority of people are actually enjoying life! There are so many lovely things to see, there is so much to do, so much fun to be had, and so many charming and interesting people to meet... How can my pen ever run dry?

TO LIGHT A FIRE

To light a fire
We must kneel.
To change a tyre,
We must descend;
To pluck a flower,
We bend;
To lift a child,
We bend again;
To touch an elder's feet
We do the same.
For prayer, or play, or just plain mending,
There's something to be said for bending!

THE INDIA I CARRIED WITH ME

A m now going back in time, to a period when I was caught between East and West, and had to make up my mind just where I belonged. I had been away from India for barely a month before I was longing to return. The insularity of the place where I found myself (Jersey, in the Channel Islands) had something to do with it, I suppose. There was little there to remind me of India or the East, not one brown face to be seen in the streets or on the beaches. I'm sure it's a different sort of place now; but fifty years ago it had nothing to offer by way of companionship or good cheer to a lonely, sensitive boy who had left home and friends in search of a 'better future'.

I had come to England with a dream of sorts, and I was to return to India with another kind of dream; but in between there were to be four years of dreary office work, lonely bed-sitting rooms, shabby lodging houses, cheap snack bars, hospital wards, and the struggle to write my first book and find a publisher for it.

I started work in a large departmental store called Le Riche. At eight in the morning, when I walked to the store, it was dark. At six in the evening, when I walked home, it was dark again.

Where were all those sunny beaches Jersey was famous for? I would have to wait for summer to see them, and a Saturday afternoon to take a dip in the sea.

Occasionally, after an early supper, I would walk along the deserted seafront. If the tide was in and the wind approaching gale-force, the waves would climb the sea wall and drench me with their cold salt spray. My aunt, with whom I was staying, thought I was quite mad to take this solitary walk; but I have always been at one with nature, even in its wilder moments, and the wind and the crashing waves gave me a sense of freedom, strengthened my determination to escape from the island and go my own way.

When I wasn't walking along the seafront, I would sit at the portable typewriter in my small attic room, and hammer out the rough chapters of the book that was to become my first novel. These were characters and incidents based on the journal I had kept during my last year in India. It was 1951, recalled in late 1952. An eighteen-year-old looking back on incidents in the life of a seventeen-year-old! Nostalgia and longing suffused those pages. How I longed to be back with my friends in the small town of Dehradun—a leafy place, sunny, fruit-laden, easygoing—every familiar corner etched clearly in my memory. Somehow, it had been that last year in Dehra that had brought me closer to the India that I had so far only taken for granted. An India of close and sometimes sentimental friendships. Of striking contrasts: a small cinema showing English pictures (a George Formby comedy or an American musical) and only a couple of hours away thousands taking a dip in the sacred water of the Ganga. Or outside the station, hundreds of pony-drawn tongas waiting to pick up passengers, while the more affluent climbed into their Ford Convertibles, Morris Minors, Baby Austins or flashy Packards and Daimlers.

But of course Dehra in the 'fifties' was a town of bicycles. Students, shopkeepers, Army cadets, office workers, all used them. The scooter (or Lambretta) had only just been invented, and it would be several years before it took over from the bicycle. It was still unaffordable for the great majority.

I was awkward on a bicycle and frequently fell off, breaking my arm on one occasion. But this did not prevent me from joining my friends on cycle rides to the Sulphur springs, or to Premnagar (where the military academy was situated) or along the Haridwar road and down to the riverbed at Lachiwala.

In Jersey, I found an old cycle belonging to my cousin, and I rode from St. Helier where we lived, to St. Brelade's Bay, at the other end of the island. But returning after dark, I was hauled up for riding without lights. I had no idea that cycles had also to be equipped with lights. Back in Dehra, we never used them!

The attic room had no view, so one of my favourite occupations, gazing out of windows, came to a stop. But perhaps this was helpful in that it made me concentrate on the sheet of paper in my typewriter. After about six months, I had a book of sorts ready for submission to any publisher who was prepared to look at it. Meanwhile, I had been through at least three jobs and had even been offered a post in the Jersey Civil Service, having successfully taken the local civil service exam—something I had done out of sheer boredom, as I had no intention of settling permanently on the island.

I had been keeping a diary of sorts and in some of the entries I had expressed my desire to get back to India, and my discontent at having to stay with relatives who were unsympathetic, not only to my feelings for India but also to my ambitions to become a writer. The diary fell into my uncle's hands. He read it, and was naturally upset. We had a row. I was contrite; but a few days later I packed my suitcases (all two of them) and stepped on to the ferry that was to take me to Southampton and then to London. Lesson one: don't leave your personal diaries lying around!

But perhaps it was all for the best, otherwise I might have hung around in Jersey for another year or two, to the detriment of my personal happiness and my writing ambitions.

I arrived in London in the middle of a thick yellow November fog—those were the days of the killer London fogs—and after a search found the students' hostel where I was given a cubicle to myself. But I did not stay there very long; the available food was awful. As soon as I got an office job—not too difficult in the 1950s—I rented an attic room in Belsize Park, the first of many bed-sitters that I was to live in during my three-year sojourn in London.

From Belsize Park I was to move to Haverstock Hill (close to Hampstead Heath), then to South London for a short time, and finally to Swiss Cottage. Most of my landladies were Jewish—refugees from persecution in pre-war Europe—and I too was a refugee of sorts, still very unsure of where I belonged. Was it England, the land of my father, or India, the land of my birth? But my father had also been born in India, had grown up and made a living there, visiting *his* father's land, England, only a couple of times during his life.

The link with Britain was tenuous, based on heredity rather than upbringing. It was more in the mind. It was a literary England I had been drawn to, not a physical England. And in fact, I took several exploratory walks around 'literary' London, visiting houses or streets where famous writers had once lived; in particular the East End and Dockland, for I had grown up on the novels and stories of Dickens, Smollett, Captain Marryat, and W.W. Jacobs. But I did not make many English friends. If they were a reserved race, I was even more reserved. Always shy, I waited for others to take the initiative. In India, people will take the initiative; they lose no time in getting to know you. Not so in England. They were too polite to look at you. And in that respect, I was more English than the English.

The gentleman who lived on the floor below me occasionally went so far as to greet me with the observation, 'Beastly weather, isn't it?'

And I would respond by saying, 'Oh, perfectly beastly,' and pass on.

How different it was when I bumped into a Gujarati boy, Praveen, who lived on the basement floor. He gave me a winning smile, and I remember saying, 'Oh, to be in Bombay now that winter's here,' and immediately we were friends.

He was only seventeen, a year or two younger than me, and he was studying at one of the polytechnics with a view to getting into the London School of Economics. At that time, most of the Indians in London were students, the great immigration rush was still a long way off, and racial antagonisms were directed more at the recently arrived West Indians than at Asians.

Praveen took me on the rounds of the coffee bars, then proliferating all over London, and introduced me to other students, among them a Vietnamese, called Thanh, who cultivated my friendship because, as he said, 'I want to speak English.' When he discovered that my accent was very un-English (you could have called it Welsh with an Anglo-Indian interaction), he dropped me like a hot brick. He was very frank, he was not interested in friendship, he said, only in improving his accent. I heard later that he'd attached himself to a young journalist from up north, who spoke broad Yorkshire.

Most evenings I remained in my room and worked on my novel. From being a journal it had become a first person narrative, and now I was turning it into fiction in the third person. The title had also undergone a few changes, but finally I settled on *The Room on the Roof.*

Into it, I put all the love and affection I felt for the friends I had left behind in Dehra. It was more than nostalgia, it was a recreation of the people, places and incidents of that last year in India. I did not want it to fade away. The riverbanks at Haridwar, the mango-groves of the Doon, the poinsettias and bougainvillaea, the games on the parade ground, the chaat shops near the Clock Tower, the summer heat, the monsoon downpours, romping naked in the rain, sitting on railway platforms, gnawing at a stick of sugar cane, listening to street cries... All this and more came crowding upon me as I sat writing before the gas fire in my little room.

When it grew very cold, I used an old overcoat given to me by Diana Athill, the junior partner at Andre Deutsch, who had promised to publish *The Room* if I rewrote it as a novel. Another who encouraged me was a BBC producer, Prudence Smith, who got me to give a couple of talks on *Radio's Third Programme*. I felt I was getting somewhere; and when I found myself confined to the Hampstead General Hospital for almost a month, with a mysterious disease which had affected the vision in my right eye, I used the left to catch up on my reading and to write a couple of short stories.

A nurse brought a tray of books around the ward every afternoon, and thanks to this courtesy, I was able to discover the delightful stories of William Saroyan and Denton Welch's sensitive first novel *Maiden Voyage*. Saroyan, a Pulitzer prizewinner for his play *The Time of Your Life*, was then very successful and popular. Denton's promising career had been cut short by a terrible accident. Out cycling on a country road, he had been knocked down by a speeding motorist. He had lived for several years, struggling against crippling injuries and almost completing his sensitive autobiography A *Voice in the Clouds*. He was thirty-one when he died. Towards the end, he could only work for three or four minutes at a time. Complications set in, and the left side of his heart started failing. Even then he made a terrific effort to finish his book. His friend Eric wrote—'Denton was upheld by the high courage which seemed somehow the fruit of his rare intelligence.'

The work of these writers, together with the bottle of Guinness I was given every day as a tonic (they had found me somewhat undernourished), meant that I walked out of the hospital with a spring in my step and a determination to succeed.

But Andre Deutsch was still dithering over my book. The firm was doing well, but he didn't like taking risks. No publisher likes losing money. And he wasn't going to make much out of my novel, a subjective and unsensational work.

But I resented his indecision. So I returned the small amount he'd paid me by way of an option, and demanded the return of my manuscript. Back came an apologetic letter and an advance (then £50) against publication.

Today, almost fifty years later, the firm of Andre Deutsch has gone, but *The Room on the Roof* is still in print, still making friends. This is not something that I gloat over, it only goes to show that books are unpredictable commodities, and that the most successful authors and publishers often fall by the wayside. Publishers go out of business, writers fade from the public mind. Even Saroyan is forgotten now. I'll be forgotten too, someday.

There were to be further delays before The *Room* was published, and I was back in India when it did come out. By then I'd almost forgotten about the book! But it picked up the John Llewellyn Rhys Prize, an award that also went to V.S. Naipaul a year later, for his first book. It was then worth only £50.

There were no big sponsors in those days. It is now sponsored by a British newspaper and is worth £5,000. This was turned down last year by another Indian writer, who disagreed with the paper's policies.

Meanwhile, in London, there were other distractions. I loved stage musicals, and if I had a little money to spare I went to the theatre, taking in such productions as *Porgy and Bess, Paint Your Wagon, Pal Joey, Teahouse of the August Moon,* and the occasional review. And of course the annual presentation of *Peter Pan* at the Scala theatre, not far from where I worked. I had grown up on *Peter Pan*, first read to me by my father in distant Jamnagar, and at school I had read Barrie's other plays and been charmed by them; but, like operetta, they had gone out of fashion and only the ageless Peter remained. 'Do you believe in fairies?' he asks in the play. And to save Tinker Bell from extinction, I clapped with the rest of the audience. But did I really believe in fairies? I looked for them in Kensington Gardens, where Peter Pan's statue stood, and found a few mothers pushing their perambulators, but no fairies. And I looked in Hyde Park, but found only courting couples. And I looked all over Leicester Square, but instead of fairies I found prostitutes soliciting business. As I was still looking for romance, I crept back to my room and my portable typewriter—I would have to create my own romance.

The small portable had been in the windows of a Jersey department store, and every time I passed the store I glanced at the window to see if the typewriter was still there. It seemed to be waiting for me to come in and take it away. I longed to buy it, partly because I had to type out the final drafts of my book, and also because it looked very dainty and attractive. It was definitely out to seduce me. Finally, with the help of a loan from Mr Bromley, a kindly senior clerk, I bought the machine. It cost only £12, but that was three month's wages at the time. It accompanied me to London, and then a couple of years later to India, giving me good service in Dehradun, New Delhi, and then Mussoorie where it finally succumbed to the damp monsoon climate.

My worldly possessions had increased, not only by the typewriter, but also by a record player which I had bought second-hand from a Thai student. I had become an ardent fan of the black singer, Eartha Kitt, and had bought all her records; but they were no good without a player until the Thai boy came to my rescue. Then the sensual, throaty voice of Eartha reverberated through the lodging house, bringing complaints from the landlady and the gentleman downstairs. I had to keep the volume low, which wasn't much fun.

I was also fond of the clarinet (turj) playing of an Indian musician, Master Ibrahim, and I had some of his recordings which transported me back to the streets and bazaars of small-town India. Light, lilting and tuneful, I preferred this sort of flute music to the warblings of the more popular songsters.

Praveen liked gangster films and wanted me to accompany him to anything which featured Humphrey Bogart, James Cagney, George Raft and other tough guys. Praveen wanted to be a tough guy himself and often struck a Bogart-like pose, cigarette dangling from the side of his mouth. There was nothing tough about Praveen, who was really rather delicate, but his affectations were charming and risible.

One day he announced that he was returning to India for a few months, as his ailing mother was anxious to see him. He asked me to come along too, to give him company during the three-week voyage. To do so, I would have to throw up my job, but I had already thrown up several jobs. They were simply stopgaps until I could establish myself as a writer. I hadn't the slightest intention or ambition of being a senior clerk or even an executive for the firm in which I was working. The only problem in leaving England then was that I would have to leave my book in limbo, as there was still no guarantee that Deutsch would publish it. But it was time I went on to write other things; time to strike out on my own, to take a chance with India. The ships were full of British and Anglo-Indian families coming to England, to make a 'better future' for themselves. I would do the opposite, go into reverse, and make my future, for good or ill, in the land of my birth.

My passport was in order, and I had only to give a week's notice to my employers. I had saved up about £200, and of this £50 went on the cost of my passage, London to Bombay. Praveen and I boarded the S.S. *Balory*, a Polish liner with a reputation for running into trouble. We had no difficulty in securing berths in tourist class. Praveen had every intention of returning to England to complete his studies. My own intentions were very vague. I knew there would be no job for me in India, but I was quietly confident that I could make a living from writing, and that too in the English language.

The *Balory* lived up to its reputation. Some of the crew went missing at Gibraltar. A passenger fell overboard in the Red Sea. Lifeboats were lowered, but he could not be found.

Praveen fell in love with an Egyptian girl who disembarked at Aden. He followed her ashore, and I had to run after him and get him back to the ship. As we docked at Ballard Pier, a fire broke out in one of the holds, but by then we were safely ashore. Praveen was swamped by relatives who carried him off to the suburbs of Bombay. I made my way to Victoria Terminus and boarded the Dehradun Express. It was a slow passenger train, which went chugging through several states in the general direction of northern India. Two days and two nights later we crawled through the eastern Doon. It was early March. The mango trees were in blossom, the peacocks were calling, and Belsize Park was far away.

MIDWINTER, DESERTED HILL STATION

I see you every day
Walk barefoot on the frozen ground.
I want to be your friend,
But you look the other way.

I see you every day
Go hungry in the bitter cold;
I'd gladly share my food,
But you look the other way.

I hear you every night
Cough desolately in the dark;
I'd share my warmth with you,
But you look the other way.

I see you every day
Pass lonely on my lonely way.
I'd gladly walk with you;
But you turn away.

HIS LAST WORDS

Seeing Ananda weeping, Gautama said,
'Do not weep, Ananda. This body of ours
Contains within itself the powers
Which renew its strength for a time
But also that which leads to its destruction.
Is there anything put together
Which shall not dissolve?'
And turning to his disciples, he said,
'When I am no longer with you,
I will still be in your midst.
You have my laws, my words, my very essence.
Beloved disciples,
If you love my memory, love one another.
I called you to tell you this.'

These were the last words of the Buddha
As he stretched himself out
And slept the final sleep
Under the great Sal tree
At Kusinagara.

THE PROSPECT OF FLOWERS

Fern Hill, The Oaks, Hunter's Lodge, The Parsonage, The Pines, Dumbarnie, Mackinnon's Hall and Windermere. These are the names of some of the old houses that still stand on the outskirts of one of the smaller Indian hill stations. Most of them have fallen into decay and ruin. They are very old, of course—built over a hundred years ago by Britons who sought relief from the searing heat of the plains. Today's visitors to the hill stations prefer to live near the markets and cinemas, and many of the old houses, set amidst oak and maple and deodar, are inhabited by wild cats, bandicoots, owls, goats and the occasional charcoal burner or mule driver.

But amongst these neglected mansions stands a neat, whitewashed cottage called Mulberry Lodge. And in it, up to a short time ago, lived an elderly English spinster named Miss Mackenzie.

In years Miss Mackenzie was more than 'elderly', being well over eighty. But no one would have guessed it. She was clean, sprightly, and wore old-fashioned but well-preserved dresses. Once a week, she walked the two miles to town to buy butter and jam and soap and sometimes a small bottle of eau de cologne.

She had lived in the hill station since she had been a girl in her teens, and that had been before the First World War. Though she had never married, she had experienced a few love affairs and was far from being the typical frustrated spinster of fiction. Her parents had been dead thirty years; her brother and sister were also dead. She had no relatives in India, and she lived on a small pension of forty rupees a month and the gift parcels that were sent out to her from New Zealand by a friend of her youth.

Like other lonely old people, she kept a pet—a large black cat with bright yellow eyes. In her small garden she grew dahlias, chrysanthemums, gladioli and a few rare orchids. She knew a great deal about plants and about wild flowers, trees, birds and insects. She had never made a serious study of these things, but having lived with them for so many years had developed an intimacy with all that grew and flourished around her.

She had few visitors. Occasionally, the padre from the local church called on her, and once a month the postman came with a letter from New Zealand or her pension papers. The milkman called every second day with a litre of milk for the lady and her cat. And sometimes she received a couple of eggs free, for the egg seller remembered a time when Miss Mackenzie, in her earlier prosperity, had bought eggs from him in large quantities. He was a sentimental man. He remembered her as a ravishing beauty in her twenties when he had gazed at her in round-eyed, nine-year-old wonder and consternation.

Now it was September and the rains were nearly over, and Miss Mackenzie's chrysanthemums were coming into their own. She hoped the coming winter wouldn't be too severe because she found it increasingly difficult to bear the cold.

One day, as she was pottering about in her garden, she saw a schoolboy plucking wild flowers on the slope above the cottage.

'Who's that?' she called. 'What are you up to, young man?'

The boy was alarmed and tried to dash up the hillside, but he slipped on pine needles and came slithering down the slope on to Miss Mackenzie's nasturtium bed.

When he found there was no escape, he gave a bright disarming smile and said, 'Good morning, miss.'

He belonged to the local English-medium school and wore a bright red blazer and a red and black striped tie. Like most polite Indian schoolboys, he called every woman 'miss'.

'Good morning,' said Miss Mackenzie severely. 'Would you mind moving out of my flower bed?'

The boy stepped gingerly over the nasturtiums and looked up at Miss Mackenzie with dimpled cheeks and appealing eyes. It was impossible to be angry with him.

'You're trespassing,' said Miss Mackenzie.

'Yes, miss.'

'And you ought to be in school at this hour.'

'Yes, miss.'

'Then what are you doing here?'

'Picking flowers, miss.' And he held up a bunch of ferns and wild flowers.

'Oh,' Miss Mackenzie was disarmed. It was a long time since she had seen a boy taking an interest in flowers, and, what was more, playing truant from school in order to gather them.

'Do you like flowers?' she asked.

'Yes, miss. I'm going to be a botan—a botantist?'

'You mean a botanist.'

'Yes, miss.'

'Well, that's unusual. Most boys at your age want to be pilots or soldiers or perhaps engineers. But you want to be a botanist. Well, well. There's still hope for the world, I see. And do you know the names of these flowers?'

'This is a bukhilo flower,' he said, showing her a small golden flower. 'That's a Pahari name. It means puja or prayer. The flower is offered during prayers. But I don't know what this is...'

He held out a pale pink flower with a soft, heart-shaped leaf.

'It's a wild begonia,' said Miss Mackenzie. 'And that purple stuff is salvia, but it isn't wild. It's a plant that escaped from my garden. Don't you have any books on flowers?'

'No, miss.'

'All right, come in and I'll show you a book.'

She led the boy into a small front room, which was crowded with furniture and books and vases and jam jars, and offered him a chair. He sat awkwardly on its edge. The black cat immediately leapt on to his knees, and settled down on them, purring loudly.

'What's your name?' asked Miss Mackenzie, as she rummaged through her books.

'Anil, miss.'

'And where do you live?'

'When school closes, I go to Delhi. My father has a business.'

'Oh, and what's that?'

'Bulbs, miss.'

'Flower bulbs?'

'No, electric bulbs.'

'Electric bulbs! You might send me a few, when you get home. Mine are always fusing, and they're so expensive, like everything else these days. Ah, here we are!' She pulled a heavy volume down from the shelf and laid it on the table. '*Flora Himaliensis*, published in 1892, and probably the only copy in India. This is a very valuable book, Anil. No other naturalist has recorded so many wild Himalayan flowers. And let me tell you this, there are many flowers and plants which are still unknown to the fancy botanists who spend all their time with microscopes instead of in the mountains. But perhaps, *you'll* do something about that, one day.'

'Yes, miss.'

They went through the book together, and Miss Mackenzie pointed out many flowers that grew in and around the hill station while the boy made notes of their names and seasons. She lit a stove, and put the kettle on for tea. And then the old English lady and the small Indian boy sat side by side over cups of hot sweet tea, absorbed in a book on wild flowers.

'May I come again?' asked Anil, when finally he rose to go.

'If you like,' said Miss Mackenzie. 'But not during school hours. You mustn't miss your classes.'

After that, Anil visited Miss Mackenzie about once a week, and nearly always brought a wild flower for her to identify. She found herself looking forward to the boy's visits—and sometimes, when more than a week passed and he didn't come, she was disappointed and lonely and would grumble at the black cat.

Anil reminded her of her brother, when the latter had been a boy. There was no physical resemblance. Andrew had been fair-haired and blue-eyed. But it was Anil's eagerness, his alert, bright look and the way he stood—legs apart, hands on hips, a picture of confidence—that reminded her of the boy who had shared her own youth in these same hills.

And why did Anil come to see her so often? Partly because she knew about wild flowers, and he really did want to become a botanist. And partly because she smelt of freshly baked bread, and that was a smell his own grandmother had possessed. And partly because she was lonely and sometimes a boy of twelve can sense loneliness better than an adult. And partly because he was a little different from other children.

By the middle of October, when there was only a fortnight

left for the school to close, the first snow had fallen on the distant mountains. One peak stood high above the rest, a white pinnacle against the azure-blue sky. When the sun set, this peak turned from orange to gold to pink to red.

'How high is that mountain?' asked Anil.

'It must be over twelve thousand feet,' said Miss Mackenzie. 'About thirty miles from here, as the crow flies. I always wanted to go there, but there was no proper road. At that height, there'll be flowers that you don't get here—the blue gentian and the purple columbine, the anemone and the edelweiss.'

'I'll go there one day,' said Anil.

'I'm sure you will, if you really want to.'

The day before his school closed, Anil came to say goodbye to Miss Mackenzie.

'I don't suppose you'll be able to find many wild flowers in Delhi,' she said. 'But have a good holiday.'

'Thank you, miss.'

As he was about to leave, Miss Mackenzie, on an impulse, thrust the *Flora Himaliensis* into his hands.

'You keep it,' she said. 'It's a present for you.'

'But I'll be back next year, and I'll be able to look at it then. It's so valuable.'

'I know it's valuable and that's why I've given it to you. Otherwise it will only fall into the hands of the junk dealers.'

'But, miss...'

'Don't argue. Besides, I may not be here next year.'

'Are you going away?'

'I'm not sure. I may go to England.'

She had no intention of going to England; she had not seen the country since she was a child, and she knew she would not fit in with the life of post-war Britain. Her home was in these hills, among the oaks and maples and deodars. It was lonely, but at her age it would be lonely anywhere.

The boy tucked the book under his arm, straightened his tie, stood stiffly to attention and said, 'Goodbye, Miss Mackenzie.' It was the first time he had spoken her name.

Winter set in early and strong winds brought rain and sleet, and soon there were no flowers in the garden or on the hillside. The cat stayed indoors, curled up at the foot of Miss Mackenzie's bed. Miss Mackenzie wrapped herself up in all her old shawls and mufflers, but still she felt the cold. Her fingers grew so stiff that she took almost an hour to open a can of baked beans. And then it snowed and for several days the milkman did not come. The postman arrived with her pension papers, but she felt too tired to take them up to town to the bank.

She spent most of the time in bed. It was the warmest place. She kept a hot-water bottle at her back, and the cat kept her feet warm. She lay in bed, dreaming of the spring and summer months. In three months' time the primroses would be out, and with the coming of spring the boy would return.

One night the hot-water bottle burst and the bedding was soaked through. As there was no sun for several days, the blanket remained damp. Miss Mackenzie caught a chill and had to keep to her cold, uncomfortable bed. She knew she had a fever but there was no thermometer with which to take her temperature. She had difficulty in breathing.

A strong wind sprang up one night, and the window flew open and kept banging all night. Miss Mackenzie was too weak to get up and close it, and the wind swept the rain and sleet into the room. The cat crept into the bed and snuggled close to its mistress's warm body. But towards morning that body had lost its warmth and the cat left the bed and started scratching about on the floor.

As a shaft of sunlight streamed through the open window,

the milkman arrived. He poured some milk into the cat's saucer on the doorstep, and the cat leapt down from the windowsill and made for the milk.

The milkman called a greeting to Miss Mackenzie, but received no answer. Her window was open and he had always known her to be up before sunrise. So he put his head in at the window and called again. But Miss Mackenzie did not answer. She had gone away to the mountain where the blue gentian and purple columbine grew.

ANGRY RIVER

In the middle of the big river, the river that began in the mountains and ended in the sea, was a small island. The river swept round the island, sometimes clawing at its banks, but never going right over it. It was over twenty years since the river had flooded the island, and at that time no one had lived there. But for the last ten years a small hut had stood there, a mud-walled hut with a sloping thatched roof. The hut had been built into a huge rock, so only three of the walls were mud, and the fourth was rock.

Goats grazed on the short grass which grew on the island, and on the prickly leaves of thorn bushes. A few hens followed them about. There was a melon patch and a vegetable patch. In the middle of the island stood a peepul tree. It was the only tree there. Even during the Great Flood, when the island had been under water, the tree had stood firm.

It was an old tree. A seed had been carried to the island by a strong wind some fifty years back, had found shelter between two rocks, had taken root there, and had sprung up to give shade and shelter to a small family; and Indians love peepul trees, especially during the hot summer months when the heart-shaped leaves catch the least breath of air and flutter eagerly, fanning those who sit beneath.

A sacred tree, the peepul: the abode of spirits, good and bad.

'Don't yawn when you are sitting beneath the tree,' Grandmother used to warn Sita.

'And if you must yawn, always snap your fingers in front of your mouth. If you forget to do that, a spirit might jump down your throat!'

'And then what will happen?' asked Sita.

'It will probably ruin your digestion,' said Grandfather, who wasn't much of a believer in spirits.

The peepul had a beautiful leaf, and Grandmother likened it to the body of the mighty god Krishna—broad at the shoulders, then tapering down to a very slim waist.

It was an old tree, and an old man sat beneath it. He was mending a fishing net. He had fished in the river for ten years, and he was a good fisherman. He knew where to find the slim silver chilwa fish and the big beautiful mahseer and the long-moustached singhara; he knew where the river was deep and where it was shallow; he knew which baits to use—which fish liked worms and which liked gram. He had taught his son to fish, but his son had gone to work in a factory in a city, nearly a hundred miles away. He had no grandson; but he had a granddaughter, Sita, and she could do all the things a boy could do, and sometimes she could do them better. She had lost her mother when she was very small. Grandmother had taught her all the things a girl should know, and she could do these as well as most girls. But neither of her grandparents could read or write, and as a result Sita couldn't read or write either.

There was a school in one of the villages across the river, but Sita had never seen it. There was too much to do on the island.

While Grandfather mended his net, Sita was inside the hut,

pressing her Grandmother's forehead, which was hot with fever. Grandmother had been ill for three days and could not eat. She had been ill before, but she had never been so bad. Grandfather had brought her some sweet oranges from the market in the nearest town, and she could suck the juice from the oranges, but she couldn't eat anything else.

She was younger than Grandfather, but because she was sick, she looked much older. She had never been very strong.

When Sita noticed that Grandmother had fallen asleep, she tiptoed out of the room on her bare feet and stood outside.

The sky was dark with monsoon clouds. It had rained all night, and in a few hours it would rain again. The monsoon rains had come early, at the end of June. Now it was the middle of July, and already the river was swollen. Its rushing sound seemed nearer and more menacing than usual.

Site went to her grandfather and sat down beside him beneath the peepul tree.

'When you are hungry, tell me,' she said, 'and I will make the bread.'

'Is your grandmother asleep?'

'She sleeps. But she will wake soon, for she has a deep pain.'

The old man stared out across the river, at the dark green of the forest, at the grey sky, and said, 'Tomorrow, if she is not better, I will take her to the hospital at Shahganj. There they will know how to make her well. You may be on your own for a few days—but you have been on your own before...'

Sita nodded gravely; she had been alone before, even during the rainy season. Now she wanted Grandmother to get well, and she knew that only Grandfather had the skill to take the small dugout boat across the river when the current was so strong. Someone would have to stay behind to look after their few possessions.

Sita was not afraid of being alone, but she did not like the look of the river. That morning, when she had gone down to fetch water, she had noticed that the level had risen. Those rocks which were normally spattered with the droppings of snipe and curlew and other water birds had suddenly disappeared.

They disappeared every year—but not so soon, surely?

'Grandfather, if the river rises, what will I do?'

'You will keep to the high ground.'

'And if the water reaches the high ground?'

'Then take the hens into the hut, and stay there.'

'And if the water comes into the hut?'

'Then climb into the peepul tree. It is a strong tree. It will not fall. And the water cannot rise higher than the tree!'

'And the goats, Grandfather?'

'I will be taking them with me, Sita. I may have to sell them to pay for good food and medicines for your grandmother. As for the hens, if it becomes necessary, put them on the roof. But do not worry too much'—and he patted Sita's head—'the water will not rise as high. I will be back soon, remember that.'

'And won't Grandmother come back?'

'Yes, of course, but they may keep her in the hospital for some time.'

◆

Towards evening, it began to rain again—big pellets of rain, scarring the surface of the river. But it was warm rain, and Sita could move about in it. She was not afraid of getting wet, she rather liked it. In the previous month, when the first monsoon shower had arrived, washing the dusty leaves of the tree and bringing up the good smell of the earth, she had exulted in it, had run about shouting for joy. She was used to it now, and indeed a little tired of the rain, but she did not mind getting wet. It was steamy indoors, and her thin dress would soon dry in the heat from the kitchen fire.

She walked about barefooted, barelegged. She was very sure on her feet; her toes had grown accustomed to gripping all kinds of rocks, slippery or sharp. And though thin, she was surprisingly strong.

Black hair streaming across her face. Black eyes. Slim brown arms. A scar on her thigh—when she was small, visiting her mother's village, a hyena had entered the house where she was sleeping, fastened on to her leg and tried to drag her away, but her screams had roused the villagers and the hyena had run off.

She moved about in the pouring rain, chasing the hens into a shelter behind the hut. A harmless brown snake, flooded out of its hole, was moving across the open ground. Sita picked up a stick, scooped the snake up, and dropped it between a cluster of rocks. She had no quarrel with snakes. They kept down the rats and the frogs. She wondered how the rats had first come to the island—probably in someone's boat, or in a sack of grain. Now it was a job to keep their numbers down.

When Sita finally went indoors, she was hungry. She ate some dried peas and warmed up some goat's milk. Grandmother woke once and asked for water, and Grandfather held the brass tumbler to her lips.

◆

It rained all night.

The roof was leaking, and a small puddle formed on the floor. They kept the kerosene lamp alight. They did not need the light, but somehow it made them feel safer.

The sound of the river had always been with them, although they were seldom aware of it; but that night they noticed a change in its sound. There was something like a moan, like a wind in the tops of tall trees and a swift hiss as the water swept round the rocks and carried away pebbles. And sometimes there was a rumble, as loose earth fell into the water.

Sita could not sleep.

She had a rag doll, made with Grandmother's help out of bits of old clothing. She kept it by her side every night. The doll was someone to talk to, when the nights were long and sleep elusive. Her grandparents were often ready to talk—and Grandmother, when she was well, was a good storyteller—but sometimes Sita wanted to have secrets, and though there were no special secrets in her life, she made up a few, because it was fun to have them. And if you have secrets, you must have a friend to share them with, a companion of one's own age. Since there were no other children on the island, Sita shared her secrets with the rag doll whose name was Mumta.

Grandfather and Grandmother were asleep, though the sound of Grandmother's laboured breathing was almost as persistent as the sound of the river.

'Mumta,' whispered Sita in the dark, starting one of her private conversations.

'Do you think Grandmother will get well again?'

Mumta always answered Sita's questions, even though the answers could only be heard by Sita.

'She is very old,' said Mumta.

'Do you think the river will reach the hut?' asked Sita.

'If it keeps raining like this, and the river keeps rising, it will reach the hut.'

'I am a little afraid of the river, Mumta. Aren't you afraid?'

'Don't be afraid. The river has always been good to us.'

'What will we do if it comes into the hut?'

'We will climb on to the roof.'

'And if it reaches the roof?'

'We will climb the peepul tree. The river has never gone higher than the peepul tree.'

As soon as the first light showed through the little skylight, Sita got up and went outside. It wasn't raining hard, it was drizzling, but it was the sort of drizzle that could continue for days, and it probably meant that heavy rain was falling in the hills where the river originated.

Sita went down to the water's edge. She couldn't find her favourite rock, the one on which she often sat dangling her feet in the water, watching the little chilwa fish swim by. It was still there, no doubt, but the river had gone over it.

She stood on the sand, and she could feel the water oozing and bubbling beneath her feet.

The river was no longer green and blue and flecked with white, but a muddy colour.

She went back to the hut. Grandfather was up now. He was getting his boat ready.

Sita milked a goat. Perhaps it was the last time she would milk it.

◆

The sun was just coming up when Grandfather pushed off in the boat. Grandmother lay in the prow. She was staring hard at Sita, trying to speak, but the words would not come. She raised her hand in a blessing.

Sita bent and touched her grandmother's feet, and then Grandfather pushed off. The little boat—with its two old people and three goats—riding swiftly on the river, moved slowly, very slowly, towards the opposite bank. The current was so swift now that Sita realized the boat would be carried about half a mile downstream before Grandfather could get it to dry land.

It bobbed about on the water, getting smaller and smaller,

until it was just a speck on the broad river.

And suddenly Sita was alone.

There was a wind, whipping the raindrops against her face; and there was the water, rushing past the island; and there was the distant shore, blurred by rain; and there was the small hut; and there was the tree.

Sita got busy. The hens had to be fed. They weren't bothered about anything except food. Sita threw them handfuls of coarse grain and potato peelings and peanut shells.

Then she took the broom and swept out the hut, lit the charcoal burner, warmed some milk, and thought, 'Tomorrow there will be no milk...' She began peeling onions. Soon her eyes started smarting and, pausing for a few moments and glancing round the quiet room, she became aware again that she was alone. Grandfather's hookah stood by itself in one corner. It was a beautiful old hookah, which had belonged to Sita's great-grandfather. The bowl was made out of a coconut encased in silver. The long winding stem was at least four feet in length. It was their most valuable possession. Grandmother's sturdy shisham-wood walking stick stood in another corner.

Sita looked around for Mumta, found the doll beneath the cot, and placed her within sight and hearing.

Thunder rolled down from the hills. BOOM—BOOM—BOOM...

'The gods of the mountains are angry,' said Sita.

'Do you think they are angry with me?'

'Why should they be angry with you?' asked Mumta.

'They don't have to have a reason for being angry. They are angry with everything, and we are in the middle of everything. We are so small—do you think they know we are here?'

'Who knows what the gods think?'

'But I made you,' said Sita, 'and I know you are here.'

'And will you save me if the river rises?'

'Yes, of course. I won't go anywhere without you, Mumta.'

Sita couldn't stay indoors for long. She went out, taking Mumta with her, and stared out across the river, to the safe land on the other side. But was it safe there? The river looked much wider now. Yes, it had crept over its banks and spread far across the flat plain. Far away, people were driving their cattle through waterlogged, flooded fields, carrying their belongings in bundles on their heads or shoulders, leaving their homes, making for the high land. It wasn't safe anywhere.

She wondered what had happened to Grandfather and Grandmother. If they had reached the shore safely, Grandfather would have to engage a bullock cart, or a pony-drawn carriage, to get Grandmother to the district town, five or six miles away, where there was a market, a court, a jail, a cinema and a hospital.

She wondered if she would ever see Grandmother again. She had done her best to look after the old lady, remembering the times when Grandmother had looked after her, had gently touched her fevered brow and had told her stories—stories about the gods: about the young Krishna, friend of birds and animals, so full of mischief, always causing confusion among the other gods; and Indra, who made the thunder and lightning; and Vishnu, the preserver of all good things, whose steed was a great white bird; and Ganesh, with the elephant's head; and Hanuman, the monkey god, who helped the young Prince Rama in his war with the King of Ceylon. Would Grandmother return to tell her more about them, or would she have to find out for herself?

The island looked much smaller now. In parts, the mud banks had dissolved quickly, sinking into the river. But in the middle of the island there was rocky ground, and the rocks would never crumble, they could only be submerged. In a space in the middle of the rocks grew the tree.

Sita climbed up the tree to get a better view. She had climbed the tree many times and it took her only a few seconds to reach the higher branches. She put her hand to her eyes to shield them from the rain, and gazed upstream.

There was water everywhere. The world had become one vast river. Even the trees on the forested side of the river looked as though they had grown from the water, like mangroves. The sky was banked with massive, moisture-laden clouds. Thunder rolled down from the hills and the river seemed to take it up with a hollow booming sound.

Something was floating down with the current, something big and bloated. It was closer now, and Sita could make out the bulky object—a drowned buffalo, being carried rapidly downstream.

So the water had already inundated the villages further upstream. Or perhaps the buffalo had been grazing too close to the rising river.

Sita's worst fears were confirmed when, a little later, she saw planks of wood, small trees and bushes, and then a wooden bedstead, floating past the island.

How long would it take for the river to reach her own small hut?

As she climbed down from the tree, it began to rain more heavily. She ran indoors, shooing the hens before her. They flew into the hut and huddled under Grandmother's cot. Sita thought it would be best to keep them together now. And having them with her took away some of the loneliness.

There were three hens and a cock bird. The river did not bother them. They were interested only in food, and Sita kept them happy by throwing them a handful of onion skins.

She would have liked to close the door and shut out the

swish of the rain and the boom of the river, but then she would have no way of knowing how fast the water rose.

She took Mumta in her arms, and began praying for the rain to stop and the river to fall. She prayed to the god Indra, and, just in case he was busy elsewhere, she prayed to other gods too. She prayed for the safety of her grandparents and for her own safety. She put herself last but only with great difficulty.

She would have to make herself a meal. So she chopped up some onions, fried them, then added turmeric and red chilli powder and stirred until she had everything sizzling; then she added a tumbler of water, some salt, and a cup of one of the cheaper lentils. She covered the pot and allowed the mixture to simmer. Doing this took Sita about ten minutes. It would take at least half an hour for the dish to be ready.

When she looked outside, she saw pools of water amongst the rocks and near the tree. She couldn't tell if it was rain water or overflow from the river.

She had an idea.

A big tin trunk stood in a corner of the room. It had belonged to Sita's mother. There was nothing in it except a cotton-filled quilt, for use during the cold weather. She would stuff the trunk with everything useful or valuable, and weigh it down so that it wouldn't be carried away—just in case the river came over the island...

Grandfather's hookah went into the trunk. Grandmother's walking stick went in too. So did a number of small tins containing the spices used in cooking—nutmeg, caraway seed, cinnamon, coriander and pepper—a bigger tin of flour and a tin of raw sugar. Even if Sita had to spend several hours in the tree, there would be something to eat when she came down again.

A clean white cotton shirt of Grandfather's, and Grandmother's only spare sari also went into the trunk. Never mind if they got stained with yellow curry powder! Never mind if they got to smell of salted fish, some of that went in too.

Sita was so busy packing the trunk that she paid no attention to the lick of cold water at her heels. She locked the trunk, placed the key high on the rock wall, and turned to give her attention to the lentils. It was only then that she discovered that she was walking about on a watery floor.

She stood still, horrified by what she saw. The water was oozing over the threshold, pushing its way into the room.

Sita was filled with panic. She forgot about her meal and everything else. Darting out of the hut, she ran splashing through ankle-deep water towards the safety of the peepul tree. If the tree hadn't been there, such a well-known landmark, she might have floundered into deep water, into the river.

She climbed swiftly into the strong arms of the tree, made herself secure on a familiar branch, and thrust the wet hair away from her eyes.

◆

She was glad she had hurried. The hut was now surrounded by water. Only the higher parts of the island could still be seen—a few rocks, the big rock on which the hut was built, a hillock on which some thorny bilberry bushes grew.

The hens hadn't bothered to leave the hut. They were probably perched on the cot now.

Would the river rise still higher? Sita had never seen it like this before. It swirled around her, stretching in all directions.

More drowned cattle came floating down. The most unusual things went by on the water—an aluminium kettle, a cane chair, a tin of tooth powder, an empty cigarette packet, a wooden slipper, a plastic doll...

A doll!

With a sinking feeling, Sita remembered Mumta.

Poor Mumta! She had been left behind in the hut. Sita, in her hurry, had forgotten her only companion.

Well, thought Sita, if I can be careless with someone I've made, how can I expect the gods to notice me, alone in the middle of the river?

The waters were higher now, the island fast disappearing.

Something came floating out of the hut.

It was an empty kerosene tin, with one of the hens perched on top. The tin came bobbing along on the water, not far from the tree, and was then caught by the current and swept into the river. The hen still managed to keep its perch.

A little later, the water must have reached the cot because the remaining hens flew up to the rock ledge and sat huddled there in the small recess.

The water was rising rapidly now, and all that remained of the island was the big rock that supported the hut, the top of the hut itself and the peepul tree.

It was a tall tree with many branches and it seemed unlikely that the water could ever go right over it. But how long would Sita have to remain there? She climbed a little higher, and as she did so, a jet-black jungle crow settled in the upper branches, and Sita saw that there was a nest in them—a crow's nest, an untidy platform of twigs wedged in the fork of a branch.

In the nest were four blue-green, speckled eggs. The crow sat on them and cawed disconsolately. But though the crow was miserable, its presence brought some cheer to Sita. At least she was not alone. Better to have a crow for company than no one at all.

Other things came floating out of the hut—a large pumpkin; a red turban belonging to Grandfather, unwinding in the water like a long snake; and then—Mumta! The doll, being filled with straw and wood shavings, moved quite swiftly on the water and passed close to the peepul tree. Sita saw it and wanted to call out, to urge her friend to make for the tree, but she knew that Mumta could not swim—the doll could only float, travel with the river, and perhaps be washed ashore many miles downstream.

The tree shook in the wind and the rain. The crow cawed and flew up, circled the tree a few times and returned to the nest. Sita clung to her branch.

The tree trembled throughout its tall frame. To Sita it felt like an earthquake tremor; she felt the shudder of the tree in her own bones.

The river swirled all around her now. It was almost up to the roof of the hut. Soon the mud walls would crumble and vanish. Except for the big rock and some trees far, far away, there was only water to be seen.

For a moment or two Sita glimpsed a boat with several people in it moving sluggishly away from the ruins of a flooded village, and she thought she saw someone pointing towards her, but the river swept them on and the boat was lost to view.

The river was very angry; it was like a wild beast, a dragon on the rampage, thundering down from the hills and sweeping across the plain, bringing with it dead animals, uprooted trees, household goods and huge fish choked to death by the swirling mud.

The tall old peepul tree groaned. Its long, winding roots clung tenaciously to the earth from which the tree had sprung many, many years ago. But the earth was softening; the stones were being washed away. The roots of the tree were rapidly losing their hold.

The crow must have known that something was wrong, because it kept flying up and circling the tree, reluctant to settle in it and reluctant to fly away. As long as the nest was there, the crow would remain, flapping about and cawing in alarm.

Sita's wet cotton dress clung to her thin body. The rain ran down from her long black hair. It poured from every leaf of the tree. The crow, too, was drenched and groggy.

The tree groaned and moved again. It had seen many monsoons. Once before, it had stood firm while the river had swirled around its massive trunk. But it had been young then. Now, old in years and tired of standing still, the tree was ready to join the river.

With a flurry of its beautiful leaves, and a surge of mud from below, the tree left its place in the earth, and, tilting, moved slowly forward, turning a little from side to side, dragging its roots along the ground. To Sita, it seemed as though the river was rising to meet the sky.

Then the tree moved into the main current of the river, and went a little faster, swinging Sita from side to side. Her feet were in the water but she clung tenaciously to her branch.

◆

The branches swayed, but Sita did not lose her grip. The water was very close now. Sita was frightened. She could not see the extent of the flood or the width of the river. She could only see the immediate danger—the water surrounding the tree.

The crow kept flying around the tree. The bird was in a terrible rage. The nest was still in the branches, but not for long... The tree lurched and twisted slightly to one side, and the nest fell into the water. Sita saw the eggs go one by one.

The crow swooped low over the water, but there was nothing it could do. In a few moments, the nest had disappeared.

The bird followed the tree for about fifty yards, as though hoping that something still remained in the tree. Then, flapping its wings, it rose high into the air and flew across the river until it was out of sight.

Sita was alone once more. But there was no time for feeling lonely. Everything was in motion—up and down and sideways and forwards. 'Any moment,' thought Sita, 'the tree will turn right over and I'll be in the water!'

She saw a turtle swimming past—a great river turtle, the kind that feeds on decaying flesh. Sita turned her face away. In the distance she saw a flooded village and people in flat-bottomed boats but they were very far away.

Because of its great size, the tree did not move very swiftly on the river. Sometimes, when it passed into shallow water, it stopped, its roots catching in the rocks; but not for long—the river's momentum soon swept it on.

At one place, where there was a bend in the river, the tree struck a sandbank and was still.

Sita felt very tired. Her arms were aching and she was no longer upright. With the tree almost on its side, she had to cling tightly to her branch to avoid falling off.

The grey weeping sky was like a great shifting dome. She knew she could not remain much longer in that position. It might be better to try swimming to some distant rooftop or tree. Then she heard someone calling.

Craning her neck to look upriver, she was able to make out a small boat coming directly towards her.

The boat approached the tree. There was a boy in the boat who held on to one of the branches to steady himself, giving his free hand to Sita. She grasped it, and slipped into the boat beside him. The boy placed his bare foot against the tree trunk and pushed away. The little boat moved swiftly down the river. The big tree was left far behind. Sita would never see it again.

◆

She lay stretched out in the boat, too frightened to talk. The boy looked at her, but he did not say anything, he did not even smile. He lay on his two small oars, stroking smoothly, rhythmically, trying to keep from going into the middle of the river. He wasn't strong enough to get the boat right out of the swift current, but he kept trying.

A small boat on a big river—a river that had no boundaries but which reached across the plains in all directions. The boat moved swiftly on the wild waters, and Sita's home was left far behind.

The boy wore only a loincloth. A sheathed knife was knotted into his waistband. He was a slim, wiry boy, with a hard flat belly; he had high cheekbones, strong white teeth. He was a little darker than Sita.

'You live on the island,' he said at last, resting on his oars and allowing the boat to drift a little, for he had reached a broader, more placid stretch of the river.

'I have seen you sometimes. But where are the others?'

'My grandmother was sick,' said Sita, 'so Grandfather took her to the hospital in Shahganj.'

'When did they leave?'

'Early this morning.'

Only that morning—and yet it seemed to Sita as though it had been many mornings ago.

'Where have you come from?' she asked. She had never seen the boy before.

'I come from...' he hesitated, '...near the foothills. I was in my boat, trying to get across the river with the news that one of the villages was badly flooded, but the current was too strong. I was swept down past your island. We cannot fight the river, we must go wherever it takes us.'

'You must be tired. Give me the oars.'

'No. There is not much to do now, except keep the boat steady.'

He brought in one oar, and with his free hand he felt under the seat where there was a small basket. He produced two mangoes, and gave one to Sita.

They bit deep into the ripe fleshy mangoes, using their teeth to tear the skin away. The sweet juice trickled down their chins. The flavour of the fruit was heavenly—truly this was the nectar of the gods!

Sita hadn't tasted a mango for over a year. For a few moments she forgot about the flood—all that mattered was the mango!

The boat drifted, but not so swiftly now, for as they went further away across the plains, the river lost much of its tremendous force.

'My name is Krishan,' said the boy. 'My father has many cows and buffaloes, but several have been lost in the flood.'

'I suppose you go to school,' said Sita.

'Yes, I am supposed to go to school. There is one not far from our village. Do you have to go to school?'

'No—there is too much work at home.'

It was no use wishing she was at home—home wouldn't be there any more—but she wished, at that moment, that she had another mango.

Towards evening, the river changed colour. The sun, low in the sky, emerged from behind the clouds, and the river changed slowly from grey to gold, from gold to a deep orange, and then, as the sun went down, all these colours were drowned in the river, and the river took on the colour of the night.

The moon was almost at the full and Sita could see across the river, to where the trees grew on its banks.

'I will try to reach the trees,' said the boy, Krishan.

'We do not want to spend the night on the water, do we?'

And so he pulled for the trees. After ten minutes of strenuous rowing, he reached a turn in the river and was able to escape the pull of the main current. Soon they were in a forest, rowing between tall evergreens.

◆

They moved slowly now, paddling between the trees, and the moon lighted their way, making a crooked silver path over the water.

'We will tie the boat to one of these trees,' said Krishan. Then we can rest. Tomorrow we will have to find our way out of the forest.'

He produced a length of rope from the bottom of the boat, tied one end to the boat's stern and threw the other end over a stout branch which hung only a few feet above the water. The boat came to rest against the trunk of the tree.

It was a tall, sturdy toon tree—the Indian mahogany—and it was quite safe, for there was no rush of water here; besides, the trees grew close together, making the earth firm and unyielding.

But the denizens of the forest were on the move.

The animals had been flooded out of their holes, caves and lairs, and were looking for shelter and dry ground.

Sita and Krishan had barely finished tying the boat to the tree when they saw a huge python gliding over the water towards them. Sita was afraid that it might try to get into the boat; but it went past them, its head above water, its great awesome length trailing behind, until it was lost in the shadows.

Krishan had more mangoes in the basket, and he and Sita sucked hungrily on them while they sat in the boat.

A big sambar stag came thrashing through the water. He did not have to swim; he was so tall that his head and shoulders remained well above the water. His antlers were big and beautiful.

'There will be other animals,' said Sita. 'Should we climb into the tree?'

'We are quite safe in the boat,' said Krishan.

'The animals are interested only in reaching dry land. They will not even hunt each other. Tonight, the deer are safe from the panther and the tiger. So lie down and sleep, and I will keep watch.'

Sita stretched herself out in the boat and closed her eyes, and the sound of the water lapping against the sides of the boat soon lulled her to sleep. She woke once, when a strange bird called overhead. She raised herself on one elbow, but Krishan was awake, sitting in the prow, and he smiled reassuringly at her. He looked blue in the moonlight, the colour of the young god Krishna, and for a few moments Sita was confused and wondered if the boy was indeed Krishna; but when she thought about it, she decided that it wasn't possible. He was just a village boy and she had seen hundreds like him—well, not exactly like him; he was different, in a way she couldn't explain to herself...

And when she slept again, she dreamt that the boy and Krishna were one, and that she was sitting beside him on a great white bird which flew over mountains, over the snow peaks of the Himalayas, into the cloudland of the gods. There was a great rumbling sound, as though the gods were angry about the whole thing, and she woke up to this terrible sound and looked about her, and there in the moonlit glade, up to his belly in water, stood a young elephant, his trunk raised as he trumpeted his predicament to the forest—for he was a young elephant, and he was lost, and he was looking for his mother.

He trumpeted again, and then lowered his head and listened. And presently, from far away, came the shrill trumpeting of another elephant. It must have been the young one's mother, because he gave several excited trumpet calls, and then went stamping and churning through the flood water towards a gap in the trees. The boat rocked in the waves made by his passing.

'It's all right now,' said Krishan. 'You can go to sleep again.'

'I don't think I will sleep now,' said Sita.

'Then I will play my flute for you,' said the boy, 'and the time will pass more quickly.'

From the bottom of the boat he took a flute, and putting it to his lips, he began to play. The sweetest music that Sita had ever heard came pouring from the little flute, and it seemed to fill the forest with its beautiful sound. And the music carried her away again, into the land of dreams, and they were riding on the bird once more, Sita and the blue god, and they were passing through clouds and mist, until suddenly the sun shot out through the clouds. And at the same moment, Sita opened her eyes and saw the sun streaming through the branches of the toon tree, its bright green leaves making a dark pattern against the blinding blue of the sky.

Sita sat up with a start, rocking the boat. There were hardly any clouds left. The trees were drenched with sunshine.

The boy Krishan was fast asleep at the bottom of the boat. His flute lay in the palm of his half-opened hand. The sun came slanting across his bare brown legs. A leaf had fallen on his upturned face, but it had not woken him, it lay on his cheek as though it had grown there.

Sita did not move again. She did not want to wake the boy. It didn't look as though the water had gone down, but it hadn't risen, and that meant the flood had spent itself.

The warmth of the sun, as it crept up Krishan's body, woke him at last. He yawned, stretched his limbs, and sat up beside Sita.

'I'm hungry,' he said with a smile.

'So am I,' said Sita.

'The last mangoes,' he said, and emptied the basket of its last two mangoes.

After they had finished the fruit, they sucked the big seeds until they were quite dry. The discarded seeds floated well on the water. Sita had always preferred them to paper boats.

'We had better move on,' said Krishan.

He rowed the boat through the trees, and then for about an hour they were passing through the flooded forest, under the dripping branches of rain-washed trees.

Sometimes they had to use the oars to push away vines and creepers. Sometimes drowned bushes hampered them. But they were out of the forest before noon.

Now the water was not very deep and they were gliding over flooded fields. In the distance they saw a village. It was on high ground. In the old days, people had built their villages on hilltops, which gave them a better defence against bandits and invading armies.

This was an old village, and though its inhabitants had long ago exchanged their swords for pruning forks, the hill on which it stood now protected it from the flood.

The people of the village—long-limbed, sturdy Jats—were generous, and gave the stranded children food and shelter. Sita was anxious to find her grandparents, and an old farmer who had business in Shahganj offered to take her there. She was hoping that Krishan would accompany her, but he said he would wait in the village, where he knew others would soon be arriving, his own people among them.

'You will be all right now,' said Krishan.

'Your grandfather will be anxious for you, so it is best that you go to him as soon as you can. And in two or three days, the water will go down and you will be able to return to the island.'

'Perhaps the island has gone forever,' said Sita.

As she climbed into the farmer's bullock cart, Krishan handed her his flute.

'Please keep it for me,' he said. 'I will come for it one day.'

And when he saw her hesitate, he added, his eyes twinkling, 'It is a good flute!'

◆

It was slow going in the bullock cart. The road was awash, the wheels got stuck in the mud, and the farmer, his grown son and Sita had to keep getting down to heave and push in order to free the big wooden wheels.

They were still in a foot or two of water. The bullocks were bespattered with mud, and Sita's legs were caked with it.

They were a day and a night in the bullock cart before they reached Shahganj; by that time, Sita, walking down the narrow bazaar of the busy market town, was hardly recognizable.

Grandfather did not recognize her. He was walking stiffly down the road, looking straight ahead of him, and would have walked right past the dusty, dishevelled girl if she had not charged straight at his thin, shaky legs and clasped him around the waist.

'Sita!' he cried, when he had recovered his wind and his balance.

'But how are you here? How did you get off the island? I was so worried—it has been very bad these last two days...'

'Is Grandmother all right?' asked Sita.

But even as she spoke, she knew that Grandmother was no longer with them. The dazed look in the old man's eyes told her as much. She wanted to cry, not for Grandmother, who could suffer no more, but for Grandfather, who looked so helpless and bewildered; she did not want him to be unhappy.

She forced back her tears, took his gnarled and trembling hand, and led him down the crowded street. And she knew, then, that it would be on her shoulder that Grandfather would have to lean in the years to come.

They returned to the island after a few days, when the river was no longer in spate. There was more rain, but the worst was over. Grandfather still had two of the goats; it had not been necessary to sell more than one.

He could hardly believe his eyes when he saw that the tree had disappeared from the island—the tree that had seemed as permanent as the island, as much a part of his life as the river itself. He marvelled at Sita's escape.

'It was the tree that saved you,' he said.

'And the boy,' said Sita.

Yes, and the boy.

She thought about the boy, and wondered if she would ever see him again. But she did not think too much, because there was so much to do.

For three nights they slept under a crude shelter made out of jute bags. During the day she helped Grandfather rebuild the mud hut. Once again, they used the big rock as a support.

The trunk which Sita had packed so carefully had not been swept off the island, but the water had got into it, and the food and clothing had been spoilt. But Grandfather's hookah had been saved, and, in the evenings, after their work was done and they had eaten the light meal which Sita prepared, he would smoke with a little of his old contentment, and tell Sita about other floods and storms which he had experienced as a boy.

Sita planted a mango seed in the same spot where the peepul tree had stood. It would be many years before it grew into a big tree, but Sita liked to imagine sitting in its branches one day, picking the mangoes straight from the tree, and feasting on them all day. Grandfather was more particular about making a vegetable garden and putting down peas, carrots, gram and mustard.

One day, when most of the hard work had been done and the new hut was almost ready, Sita took the flute which had been given to her by the boy, and walked down to the water's edge and tried to play it.

But all she could produce were a few broken notes, and even the goats paid no attention to her music.

Sometimes, Sita thought she saw a boat coming down the river and she would run to meet it; but usually there was no boat, or if there was, it belonged to a stranger or to another fisherman. And so she stopped looking out for boats. Sometimes she thought she heard the music of a flute, but it seemed very distant and she could never tell where the music came from.

Slowly, the rains came to an end. The flood waters had receded, and in the villages people were beginning to till the land again and sow crops for the winter months. There were cattle fairs and wrestling matches. The days were warm and sultry. The water in the river was no longer muddy, and one evening Grandfather brought home a huge mahseer fish and Sita made it into a delicious curry.

♦

Grandfather sat outside the hut, smoking his hookah. Sita was at the far end of the island, spreading clothes on the rocks to dry. One of the goats had followed her. It was the friendlier of the two, and often followed Sita about the island. She had made it a necklace of coloured beads.

She sat down on a smooth rock, and, as she did so, she noticed a small bright object in the sand near her feet. She stooped and picked it up. It was a little wooden toy—a coloured peacock—that must have come down on the river and been swept ashore on the island. Some of the paint had rubbed off, but for Sita, who had no toys, it was a great find. Perhaps it would speak to her, as Mumta had spoken to her.

As she held the toy peacock in the palm of her hand, she thought she heard the flute music again, but she did not look up. She had heard it before, and she was sure that it was all in her mind. But this time the music sounded nearer, much nearer. There was a soft footfall in the sand. And, looking up, she saw the boy, Krishan, standing over her.

'I thought you would never come,' said Sita.

'I had to wait until the rains were over. Now that I am free, I will come more often. Did you keep my flute?'

'Yes, but I cannot play it properly. Sometimes it plays by itself, I think, but it will not play for me!'

'I will teach you to play it,' said Krishan.

He sat down beside her, and they cooled their feet in the water, which was clear now, reflecting the blue of the sky. You could see the sand and the pebbles of the riverbed.

'Sometimes the river is angry, and sometimes it is kind,' said Sita.

'We are part of the river,' said the boy.

'We cannot live without it.'

It was a good river, deep and strong, beginning in the mountains and ending in the sea. Along its banks, for hundreds of miles, lived millions of people, and Sita was only one small girl among them, and no one had ever heard of her, no one knew her—except for the old man, the boy and the river.

GRANDFATHER FIGHTS AN OSTRICH

Before my grandfather joined the Indian Railways, he worked for a few years on the East African Railways, and it was during that period that he had his now famous encounter with the ostrich. My childhood was frequently enlivened by this oft-told tale of his, and I give it here in his own words—or as well as I can remember them!

While engaged in the laying of a new railway line, I had a miraculous escape from an awful death. I lived in a small township, but my work lay some twelve miles away, and I had to go to the work site and back on horseback.

One day, my horse had a slight accident, so I decided to do the journey on foot, being a great walker in those days. I also knew of a short cut through the hills that would save me about six miles. This short cut went through an ostrich farm—or 'camp', as it was called. It was the breeding season. I was fairly familiar with the ways of ostriches, and knew that male birds were very aggressive in the breeding season, ready to attack on the slightest provocation, but I also knew that my dog would scare away any bird that might try to attack me.

Strange though it may seem, even the biggest ostrich (and some of them grow to a height of nine feet) will run faster than a racehorse at the sight of even a small dog. So, I felt quite safe in the company of my dog, a mongrel who had adopted me some two months previously.

On arrival at the 'camp', I climbed through the wire fencing and, keeping a good lookout, dodged across the open spaces between the thorn bushes. Now and then I caught a glimpse of the birds feeding some distance away.

I had gone about half a mile from the fencing when up started a hare. In an instant my dog gave chase. I tried calling him back, even though I knew it was hopeless. Chasing hares was that dog's passion.

I don't know whether it was the dog's bark or my own shouting, but what I was most anxious to avoid immediately happened. The ostriches were startled and began darting to and fro. Suddenly, I saw a big male bird emerge from a thicket about a hundred yards away. He stood still and stared at me for a few moments. I stared back. Then, expanding his short wings and with his tail erect, he came bounding towards me.

As I had nothing, not even a stick, with which to defend myself, I turned and ran towards the fence. But it was an unequal race. What were my steps of two or three feet against the creature's great strides of sixteen to twenty feet? There was only one hope: to get behind a large bush and try to elude the bird until help came. A dodging game was my only chance.

And so, I rushed for the nearest clump of thorn bushes and waited for my pursuer. The great bird wasted no time—he was immediately upon me.

Then the strangest encounter took place. I dodged this way and that, taking great care not to get directly in front of the ostrich's deadly kick. Ostriches kick forward, and with such terrific force that if you were struck, their huge chisel-like nails would cause you much damage.

I was breathless, and really quite helpless, calling wildly for help as I circled the thorn bush. My strength was ebbing. How much longer could I keep going? I was ready to drop from exhaustion. As if aware of my condition, the infuriated bird suddenly doubled back on his course and charged straight at me. With a desperate effort I managed to step to one side. I don't know how, but I found myself holding on to one of the creature's wings, quite close to its body.

It was now the ostrich's turn to be frightened. He began to turn, or rather waltz, moving round and round so quickly that my feet were soon swinging out from his body, almost horizontally! All the while the ostrich kept opening and shutting his beak with loud snaps.

Imagine my situation as I clung desperately to the wing of the enraged bird. He was whirling me round and round as though he were a discus thrower—and I the discus! My arms soon began to ache with the strain, and the swift and continuous circling was making me dizzy. But I knew that if I relaxed my hold, even for a second, a terrible fate awaited me.

Round and round we went in a great circle. It seemed as if that spiteful bird would never tire. And, I knew I could not hold on much longer. Suddenly the ostrich went into reverse! This unexpected move made me lose my hold and sent me sprawling to the ground. I landed in a heap near the thorn bush and in an instant, before I even had time to realize what had happened, the big bird was upon me. I thought the end had come. Instinctively I raised my hands to protect my face. But the ostrich did not strike.

I moved my hands from my face and there stood the creature with one foot raised, ready to deliver a deadly kick! I couldn't move. Was the bird going to play cat-and-mouse with me, and prolong the agony?

As I watched, frightened and fascinated, the ostrich turned his head sharply to the left. A second later, he jumped back, turned, and made off as fast as he could go. Dazed, I wondered what had happened to make him beat so unexpected a retreat.

I soon found out. To my great joy, I heard the bark of my truant dog, and the next moment he was jumping around me, licking my face and hands. Needless to say, I returned his caresses most affectionately! And, I took good care to see that he did not leave my side until we were well clear of that ostrich 'camp'.

THE BLUE UMBRELLA

I

'Neelu! Neelu!' cried Binya.

She scrambled barefoot over the rocks, ran over the short summer grass, up and over the brow of the hill, all the time calling 'Neelu, Neelu!' Neelu—Blue—was the name of the blue-grey cow. The other cow, which was white, was called Gori, meaning Fair One. They were fond of wandering off on their own, down to the stream or into the pine forest, and sometimes they came back by themselves and sometimes they stayed away—almost deliberately, it seemed to Binya.

If the cows didn't come home at the right time, Binya would be sent to fetch them. Sometimes her brother, Bijju, went with her, but these days he was busy preparing for his exams and didn't have time to help with the cows.

Binya liked being on her own, and sometimes she allowed the cows to lead her into some distant valley, and then they would all be late coming home. The cows preferred having Binya with them, because she let them wander. Bijju pulled them by their tails if they went too far.

Binya belonged to the mountains, to this part of the

Himalayas known as Garhwal. Dark forests and lonely hilltops held no terrors for her. It was only when she was in the market town, jostled by the crowds in the bazaar, that she felt rather nervous and lost. The town, five miles from the village, was also a pleasure resort for tourists from all over India.

Binya was probably ten. She may have been nine or even eleven, she couldn't be sure because no one in the village kept birthdays; but her mother told her she'd been born during a winter when the snow had come up to the windows, and that was just over ten years ago, wasn't it? Two years later, her father had died, but his passing had made no difference to their way of life. They had three tiny terraced fields on the side of the mountain, and they grew potatoes, onions, ginger, beans, mustard and maize: not enough to sell in the town, but enough to live on.

Like most mountain girls, Binya was quite sturdy, fair of skin, with pink cheeks and dark eyes and her black hair tied in a pigtail. She wore pretty glass bangles on her wrists, and a necklace of glass beads. From the necklace hung a leopard's claw. It was a lucky charm, and Binya always wore it. Bijju had one, too, only his was attached to a string.

Binya's full name was Binyadevi, and Bijju's real name was Vijay, but everyone called them Binya and Bijju. Binya was two years younger than her brother.

She had stopped calling for Neelu; she had heard the cowbells tinkling, and knew the cows hadn't gone far. Singing to herself, she walked over fallen pine needles into the forest glade on the spur of the hill. She heard voices, laughter, the clatter of plates and cups, and stepping through the trees, she came upon a party of picnickers.

They were holidaymakers from the plains. The women were dressed in bright saris, the men wore light summer shirts, and the children had pretty new clothes. Binya, standing in the shadows between the trees, went unnoticed; for some time she watched the picnickers, admiring their clothes, listening to their unfamiliar accents, and gazing rather hungrily at the sight of all their food. And then her gaze came to rest on a bright blue umbrella, a frilly thing for women, which lay open on the grass beside its owner.

Now Binya had seen umbrellas before, and her mother had a big black umbrella which nobody used anymore because the field rats had eaten holes in it, but this was the first time Binya had seen such a small, dainty, colourful umbrella and she fell in love with it. The umbrella was like a flower, a great blue flower that had sprung up on the dry brown hillside.

She moved forward a few paces so that she could see the umbrella better. As she came out of the shadows into the sunlight, the picnickers saw her.

'Hello, look who's here!' exclaimed the older of the two women. 'A little village girl!'

'Isn't she pretty?' remarked the other. 'But how torn and dirty her clothes are!' It did not seem to bother them that Binya could hear and understand everything they said about her.

'They're very poor in the hills,' said one of the men.

'Then let's give her something to eat.' And the older woman beckoned to Binya to come closer.

Hesitantly, nervously, Binya approached the group.

Normally she would have turned and fled, but the attraction was the pretty blue umbrella. It had cast a spell over her, drawing her forward almost against her will.

'What's that on her neck?' asked the younger woman.

'A necklace of sorts.'

'It's a pendant—see, there's a claw hanging from it!'

'It's a tiger's claw,' said the man beside her. (He had never seen a tiger's claw.) 'A lucky charm. These people wear them to keep away evil spirits.' He looked to Binya for confirmation, but Binya said nothing.

'Oh, I want one too!' said the woman, who was obviously his wife.

'You can't get them in shops.'

'Buy hers, then. Give her two or three rupees, she's sure to need the money.'

The man, looking slightly embarrassed but anxious to please his young wife, produced a two-rupee note and offered it to Binya, indicating that he wanted the pendant in exchange. Binya put her hand to the necklace, half afraid that the excited woman would snatch it away from her. Solemnly she shook her head.

The man then showed her a five-rupee note, but again, Binya shook her head.

'How silly she is!' exclaimed the young woman.

'It may not be hers to sell,' said the man. 'But I'll try again. How much do you want—what can we give you?' And he waved his hand towards the picnic things scattered about on the grass.

Without any hesitation, Binya pointed to the umbrella.

'My umbrella!' exclaimed the young woman. 'She wants my umbrella. What cheek!'

'Well, you want her pendant, don't you?'

'That's different.'

'Is it?'

The man and his wife were beginning to quarrel with each other.

'I'll ask her to go away,' said the older woman.

'We're making such fools of ourselves.'

'But I want the pendant!' cried the other, petulantly.

And then, on an impulse, she picked up the umbrella and held it out to Binya.

'Here, take the umbrella!'

Binya removed her necklace and held it out to the young woman, who immediately placed it around her own neck. Then, Binya took the umbrella and held it up. It did not look so small in her hands; in fact, it was just the right size.

She had forgotten about the picnickers, who were busy examining the pendant. She turned the blue umbrella this way and that, looked through the bright blue silk at the pulsating sun, and then, still keeping it open, turned and disappeared into the forest glade.

II

Binya seldom closed the blue umbrella. Even when she had it in the house, she left it lying open in a corner of the room. Sometimes Bijju snapped it shut, complaining that it got in the way. She would open it again a little later. It wasn't beautiful when it was closed.

Whenever Binya went out—whether it was to graze the cows, or fetch water from the spring, or carry milk to the little tea shop on the Tehri road—she took the umbrella with her. That patch of sky-blue silk could always be seen on the hillside.

Old Ram Bharosa (Ram the Trustworthy) kept the tea shop on the Tehri road. It was a dusty, un-metalled road. Once a day, the Tehri bus stopped near his shop and passengers got down to sip hot tea or drink a glass of curd. He kept a few bottles of Coca-Cola too, but as there was no ice, the bottles got hot in the sun and so were seldom opened. He also kept sweets and toffees, and when Binya or Bijju had a few coins to spare, they would spend them at the shop. It was only a mile from the village.

Ram Bharosa was astonished to see Binya's blue umbrella. 'What have you there, Binya?' he asked.

Binya gave the umbrella a twirl and smiled at Ram Bharosa. She was always ready with her smile, and would willingly have lent it to anyone who was feeling unhappy.

'That's a lady's umbrella,' said Ram Bharosa. 'That's only for memsahibs. Where did you get it?'

'Someone gave it to me—for my necklace.'

'You exchanged it for your lucky claw!'

Binya nodded.

'But what do you need it for? The sun isn't hot enough, and it isn't meant for the rain. It's just a pretty thing for rich ladies to play with!'

Binya nodded and smiled again. Ram Bharosa was quite right; it was just a beautiful plaything. And that was exactly why she had fallen in love with it.

'I have an idea,' said the shopkeeper. 'It's no use to you, that umbrella. Why not sell it to me? I'll give you five rupees for it.'

'It's worth fifteen,' said Binya.

'Well, then, I'll give you ten.'

Binya laughed and shook her head.

'Twelve rupees?' said Ram Bharosa, but without much hope.

Binya placed a five-paise coin on the counter.

'I came for a toffee,' she said.

Ram Bharosa pulled at his drooping whiskers, gave Binya a wry look, and placed a toffee in the palm of her hand. He watched Binya as she walked away along the dusty road. The blue umbrella held him fascinated, and he stared after it until it was out of sight.

The villagers used this road to go to the market town. Some used the bus, a few rode on mules and most people walked. Today, everyone on the road turned their heads to stare at the girl with the bright blue umbrella.

Binya sat down in the shade of a pine tree. The umbrella,

still open, lay beside her. She cradled her head in her arms, and presently she dozed off. It was that kind of day, sleepily warm and summery.

And while she slept, a wind sprang up.

It came quietly, swishing gently through the trees, humming softly. Then it was joined by other random gusts, bustling over the tops of the mountains. The trees shook their heads and came to life. The wind fanned Binya's cheeks. The umbrella stirred on the grass.

The wind grew stronger, picking up dead leaves and sending them spinning and swirling through the air. It got into the umbrella and began to drag it over the grass. Suddenly it lifted the umbrella and carried it about six feet from the sleeping girl. The sound woke Binya.

She was on her feet immediately, and then she was leaping down the steep slope. But just as she was within reach of the umbrella, the wind picked it up again and carried it further downhill.

Binya set off in pursuit. The wind was in a wicked, playful mood. It would leave the umbrella alone for a few moments but as soon as Binya came near, it would pick up the umbrella again and send it bouncing, floating, dancing away from her.

The hill grew steeper. Binya knew that after twenty yards it would fall away in a precipice. She ran faster. And the wind ran with her, ahead of her, and the blue umbrella stayed up with the wind.

A fresh gust picked it up and carried it to the very edge of the cliff. There it balanced for a few seconds, before toppling over, out of sight.

Binya ran to the edge of the cliff. Going down on her hands and knees, she peered down the cliff face. About a hundred feet below, a small stream rushed between great boulders. Hardly anything grew on the cliff face—just a few stunted bushes, and, halfway down, a wild cherry tree growing crookedly out of the rocks and hanging across the chasm. The umbrella had stuck in the cherry tree.

Binya didn't hesitate. She may have been timid with strangers, but she was at home on a hillside. She stuck her bare leg over the edge of the cliff and began climbing down. She kept her face to the hillside, feeling her way with her feet, only changing her handhold when she knew her feet were secure. Sometimes she held on to the thorny bilberry bushes, but she did not trust the other plants, which came away very easily.

Loose stones rattled down the cliff. Once on their way, the stones did not stop until they reached the bottom of the hill; and they took other stones with them, so that there was soon a cascade of stones, and Binya had to be very careful not to start a landslide.

As agile as a mountain goat, she did not take more than five minutes to reach the crooked cherry tree. But the most difficult task remained—she had to crawl along the trunk of the tree, which stood out at right angles from the cliff. Only by doing this could she reach the trapped umbrella.

Binya felt no fear when climbing trees. She was proud of the fact that she could climb them as well as Bijju. Gripping the rough cherry bark with her toes, and using her knees as leverage, she crawled along the trunk of the projecting tree until she was almost within reach of the umbrella. She noticed with dismay that the blue cloth was torn in a couple of places.

She looked down, and it was only then that she felt afraid. She was right over the chasm, balanced precariously about eighty feet above the boulder-strewn stream. Looking down, she felt quite dizzy. Her hands shook, and the tree shook too. If she slipped now, there was only one direction in which she could fall—down, down, into the depths of that dark and shadowy ravine.

There was only one thing to do; concentrate on the patch of blue just a couple of feet away from her. She did not look down or up, but straight ahead, and willing herself forward, she managed to reach the umbrella.

She could not crawl back with it in her hands. So, after dislodging it from the forked branch in which it had stuck, she let it fall, still open, into the ravine below.

Cushioned by the wind, the umbrella floated serenely downwards, landing in a thicket of nettles.

Binya crawled back along the trunk of the cherry tree. Twenty minutes later, she emerged from the nettle clump, her precious umbrella held aloft. She had nettle stings all over her legs, but she was hardly aware of the smarting. She was as immune to nettles as Bijju was to bees.

III

About four years previously, Bijju had knocked a hive out of an oak tree, and had been badly stung on the face and legs. It had been a painful experience. But now, if a bee stung him, he felt nothing at all: he had been immunized for life!

He was on his way home from school. It was two o'clock and he hadn't eaten since six in the morning. Fortunately, the kingora bushes—the bilberries—were in fruit, and already Bijju's lips were stained purple with the juice of the wild, sour fruit.

He didn't have any money to spend at Ram Bharosa's shop, but he stopped there anyway to look at the sweets in their glass jars.

'And what will you have today?' asked Ram Bharosa.

'No money,' said Bijju.

'You can pay me later.'

Bijju shook his head. Some of his friends had taken sweets on credit, and at the end of the month they had found they'd eaten more sweets than they could possibly pay for! As a result, they'd had to hand over to Ram Bharosa some of their most treasured possessions—such as a curved knife for cutting grass, or a small hand-axe, or a jar for pickles, or a pair of earrings—and these had become the shopkeeper's possessions and were kept by him or sold in his shop.

Ram Bharosa had set his heart on having Binya's blue umbrella, and so naturally he was anxious to give credit to either of the children, but so far neither had fallen into the trap.

Bijju moved on, his mouth full of Kingora berries. Halfway home, he saw Binya with the cows. It was late evening, and the sun had gone down, but Binya still had the umbrella open. The two small rents had been stitched up by her mother.

Bijju gave his sister a handful of berries. She handed him the umbrella while she ate the berries.

'You can have the umbrella until we get home,' she said. It was her way of rewarding Bijju for bringing her the wild fruit.

Calling 'Neelu! Gori!' Binya and Bijju set out for home, followed at some distance by the cows.

It was dark before they reached the village, but Bijju still had the umbrella open.

◆

Most of the people in the village were a little envious of Binya's blue umbrella. No one else had ever possessed one like it. The schoolmaster's wife thought it was quite wrong for a poor cultivator's daughter to have such a fine umbrella while she, a second-class BA, had to make do with an ordinary black one. Her husband offered to have their old umbrella dyed blue; she gave him a scornful look, and loved him a little less than before. The pujari, who looked after the temple, announced that he would buy a multi-coloured umbrella the next time he was in the town. A few days later he returned looking annoyed and grumbling that they weren't available except in Delhi. Most people consoled themselves by saying that Binya's pretty umbrella wouldn't keep out the rain, if it rained heavily; that it would shrivel in the sun, if the sun was fierce; that it would collapse in a wind, if the wind was strong; that it would attract lightning, if lightning fell near it; and that it would prove unlucky, if there was any ill luck going about. Secretly, everyone admired it.

Unlike the adults, the children didn't have to pretend. They were full of praise for the umbrella. It was so light, so pretty, so bright a blue! And it was just the right size for Binya. They knew that if they said nice things about the umbrella, Binya would smile and give it to them to hold for a little while—just a very little while!

Soon it was the time of the monsoon. Big black clouds kept piling up, and thunder rolled over the hills.

Binya sat on the hillside all afternoon, waiting for the rain. As soon as the first big drop of rain came down, she raised the umbrella over her head. More drops, big ones, came pattering down. She could see them through the umbrella silk, as they broke against the cloth.

And then there was a cloudburst, and it was like standing under a waterfall. The umbrella wasn't really a rain umbrella, but it held up bravely. Only Binya's feet got wet. Rods of rain fell around her in a curtain of shivered glass.

Everywhere on the hillside people were scurrying for shelter. Some made for a charcoal burner's hut, others for a mule-shed, or Ram Bharosa's shop. Binya was the only one who didn't run. This was what she'd been waiting for—rain on her umbrella—and she wasn't in a hurry to go home. She didn't mind getting her feet wet. The cows didn't mind getting wet either.

Presently she found Bijju sheltering in a cave. He would have enjoyed getting wet, but he had his schoolbooks with him and he couldn't afford to let them get spoilt. When he saw Binya, he came out of the cave and shared the umbrella. He was a head taller than his sister, so he had to hold the umbrella for her, while she held his books.

The cows had been left far behind.

'Neelu, Neelu!' called Binya.

'Gori!' called Bijju.

When their mother saw them sauntering home through the driving rain, she called out, 'Binya! Bijju! Hurry up, and bring the cows in! What are you doing out there in the rain?'

'Just testing the umbrella,' said Bijju.

IV

The rains set in, and the sun only made brief appearances. The hills turned a lush green. Ferns sprang up on walls and tree trunks. Giant lilies reared up like leopards from the tall grass. A white mist coiled and uncoiled as it floated up from the valley. It was a beautiful season, except for the leeches.

Every day, Binya came home with a couple of leeches fastened to the flesh of her bare legs. They fell off by themselves just as soon as they'd had their thimbleful of blood, but you didn't know they were on you until they fell off, and then, later, the skin became very sore and itchy. Some of the older people still believed that to be bled by leeches was a remedy for various ailments. Whenever Ram Bharosa had a headache, he applied a leech to his throbbing temple.

Three days of incessant rain had flooded out a number of small animals who lived in holes in the ground. Binya's mother suddenly found the roof full of field rats. She had to drive them out; they ate too much of her stored-up wheat flour and rice. Bijju liked lifting up large rocks to disturb the scorpions who were sleeping beneath. And snakes came out to bask in the sun.

Binya had just crossed the small stream at the bottom of the hill when she saw something gliding out of the bushes and coming towards her. It was a long black snake. A clatter of loose stones frightened it. Seeing the girl in its way, it rose up, hissing, prepared to strike. The forked tongue darted out, the venomous head lunged at Binya.

Binya's umbrella was open as usual. She thrust it forward, between herself and the snake, and the snake's hard snout thudded twice against the strong silk of the umbrella. The reptile then turned and slithered away over the wet rocks, disappearing into a clump of ferns.

Binya forgot about the cows and ran all the way home to tell her mother how she had been saved by the umbrella. Bijju had to put away his books and go out to fetch the cows. He carried a stout stick, in case he met with any snakes.

♦

First the summer sun, and now the endless rain, meant that the umbrella was beginning to fade a little. From a bright blue it had changed to a light blue. But it was still a pretty thing, and tougher than it looked, and Ram Bharosa still desired it. He did not want to sell it; he wanted to own it. He was probably the richest man in the area—so why shouldn't he have a blue umbrella? Not a day passed without his getting a glimpse of Binya and the umbrella; and the more he saw the umbrella, the more he wanted it.

The schools closed during the monsoon, but this didn't mean that Bijju could sit at home doing nothing. Neelu and Gori were providing more milk than was required at home, so

Binya's mother was able to sell a kilo of milk every day—half a kilo to the schoolmaster, and half a kilo (at reduced rate) to the temple pujari. Bijju had to deliver the milk every morning.

Ram Bharosa had asked Bijju to work in his shop during the holidays, but Bijju didn't have time—he had to help his mother with the ploughing and the transplanting of the rice seedlings. So Ram Bharosa employed a boy from the next village, a boy called Rajaram. He did all the washing-up, and ran various errands. He went to the same school as Bijju, but the two boys were not friends.

One day, as Binya passed the shop, twirling her blue umbrella, Rajaram noticed that his employer gave a deep sigh and began muttering to himself.

'What's the matter, Babuji?' asked the boy.

'Oh, nothing,' said Ram Bharosa. 'It's just a sickness that has come upon me. And it's all due to that girl Binya and her wretched umbrella.'

'Why, what has she done to you?'

'Refused to sell me her umbrella! There's pride for you. And I offered her ten rupees.'

'Perhaps, if you gave her twelve...'

'But it isn't new any longer. It isn't worth eight rupees now. All the same, I'd like to have it.'

'You wouldn't make a profit on it,' said Rajaram.

'It's not the profit I'm after, wretch! It's the thing itself. It's the beauty of it!'

'And what would you do with it, Babuji? You don't visit anyone—you're seldom out of your shop. Of what use would it be to you?'

'Of what use is a poppy in a cornfield? Of what use is a rainbow? Of what use are you, numbskull? Wretch! I, too, have a soul. I want the umbrella, because—because I want its beauty to be mine!'

Rajaram put the kettle on to boil, began dusting the counter, all the time muttering, 'I'm as useful as an umbrella,' and then, after a short period of intense thought, said, 'What will you give me, Babuji, if I get the umbrella for you?'

'What do you mean?' asked the old man.

'You know what I mean. What will you give me?'

'You mean to steal it, don't you, you wretch? What a delightful child you are! I'm glad you're not my son or my enemy. But look, everyone will know it has been stolen, and then how will I be able to show off with it?'

'You will have to gaze upon it in secret,' said Rajaram with a chuckle. 'Or take it into Tehri, and have it coloured red! That's your problem. But tell me, Babuji, do you want it badly enough to pay me three rupees for stealing it without being seen?'

Ram Bharosa gave the boy a long, sad look. 'You're a sharp boy,' he said. 'You'll come to a bad end. I'll give you two rupees.'

'Three,' said the boy.

'Two,' said the old man.

'You don't really want it, I can see that,' said the boy.

'Wretch!' said the old man. 'Evil one! Darkener of my doorstep! Fetch me the umbrella, and I'll give you three rupees.'

V

Binya was in the forest glade where she had first seen the umbrella. No one came there for picnics during the monsoon. The grass was always wet and the pine needles were slippery underfoot. The tall trees shut out the light, and poisonous-looking mushrooms, orange and purple, sprang up everywhere. But it was a good place for porcupines, who seemed to like the mushrooms, and Binya was searching for porcupine quills.

The hill people didn't think much of porcupine quills, but

far away in southern India, the quills were valued as charms and sold at a rupee each. So Ram Bharosa paid a tenth of a rupee for each quill brought to him, and he in turn sold the quills at a profit to a trader from the plains.

Binya had already found five quills, and she knew there'd be more in the long grass. For once, she'd put her umbrella down. She had to put it aside if she was to search the ground thoroughly.

It was Rajaram's chance.

He'd been following Binya for some time, concealing himself behind trees and rocks, creeping closer whenever she became absorbed in her search. He was anxious that she should not see him and be able to recognize him later.

He waited until Binya had wandered some distance from the umbrella. Then, running forward at a crouch, he seized the open umbrella and dashed off with it.

But Rajaram had very big feet. Binya heard his heavy footsteps and turned just in time to see him as he disappeared between the trees. She cried out, dropped the porcupine quills, and gave chase.

Binya was swift and sure-footed, but Rajaram had a long stride. All the same, he made the mistake of running downhill. A long-legged person is much faster going uphill than down. Binya reached the edge of the forest glade in time to see the thief scrambling down the path to the stream. He had closed the umbrella so that it would not hinder his flight.

Binya was beginning to gain on the boy. He kept to the path, while she simply slid and leapt down the steep hillside. Near the bottom of the hill the path began to straighten out, and it was here that the long-legged boy began to forge ahead again.

Bijju was coming home from another direction. He had a bundle of sticks which he'd collected for the kitchen fire. As he reached the path, he saw Binya rushing down the hill as though all the mountain spirits in Garhwal were after her.

'What's wrong?' he called. 'Why are you running?'

Binya paused only to point at the fleeing Rajaram.

'My umbrella!' she cried. 'He has stolen it!'

Bijju dropped his bundle of sticks, and ran after his sister. When he reached her side, he said, 'I'll soon catch him!' and went sprinting away over the lush green grass. He was fresh, and he was soon well ahead of Binya and gaining on the thief.

Rajaram was crossing the shallow stream when Bijju caught up with him. Rajaram was the taller boy, but Bijju was much stronger. He flung himself at the thief, caught him by the legs, and brought him down in the water. Rajaram got to his feet and tried to drag himself away, but Bijju still had him by a leg. Rajaram overbalanced and came down with a great splash. He had let the umbrella fall. It began to float away on the current. Just then Binya arrived, flushed and breathless, and went dashing into the stream after the umbrella.

Meanwhile, a tremendous fight was taking place. Locked in fierce combat, the two boys swayed together on a rock, tumbled on to the sand, rolled over and over the pebbled bank until they were again thrashing about in the shallows of the stream. The magpies, bulbuls and other birds were disturbed, and flew away with cries of alarm.

Covered with mud, gasping and spluttering, the boys groped for each other in the water. After five minutes of frenzied struggle, Bijju emerged victorious.

Rajaram lay flat on his back on the sand, exhausted, while Bijju sat astride him, pinning him down with his arms and legs.

'Let me get up!' gasped Rajaram. 'Let me go—I don't want your useless umbrella!'

'Then why did you take it?' demanded Bijju. 'Come on—tell me why!'

'It was that skinflint Ram Bharosa,' said Rajaram.
'He told me to get it for him. He said if I didn't fetch it, I'd lose my job.'

VI

By early October, the rains were coming to an end. The leeches disappeared. The ferns turned yellow, and the sunlight on the green hills was mellow and golden, like the limes on the small tree in front of Binya's home. Bijju's days were happy ones as he came home from school, munching on roasted corn. Binya's umbrella had turned a pale milky blue, and was patched in several places, but it was still the prettiest umbrella in the village, and she still carried it with her wherever she went.

The cold, cruel winter wasn't far off, but somehow October seems longer than other months, because it is a kind month: the grass is good to be upon, the breeze is warm and gentle and pine-scented. That October, everyone seemed contented—everyone, that is, except Ram Bharosa.

The old man had by now given up all hope of ever possessing Binya's umbrella. He wished he had never set eyes on it. Because of the umbrella, he had suffered the tortures of greed, the despair of loneliness. Because of the umbrella, people had stopped coming to his shop!

Ever since it had become known that Ram Bharosa tried to have the umbrella stolen, the village people had turned against him. They stopped trusting the old man, instead of buying their soap and tea and matches from his shop, they preferred to walk an extra mile to the shops near the Tehri bus stand. Who would have dealings with a man who had sold his soul for an umbrella? The children taunted him, twisted his name around. From 'Ram the Trustworthy' he became 'Trusty Umbrella Thief'.

The old man sat alone in his empty shop, listening to the eternal hissing of his kettle and wondering if anyone would ever again step in for a glass of tea. Ram Bharosa had lost his own appetite, and ate and drank very little. There was no money coming in. He had his savings in a bank in Tehri, but it was a terrible thing to have to dip into them! To save money, he had dismissed the blundering Rajaram. So he was left without any company. The roof leaked and the wind got in through the corrugated tin sheets, but Ram Bharosa didn't care.

Bijju and Binya passed his shop almost every day. Bijju went by with a loud but tuneless whistle. He was one of the world's whistlers; cares rested lightly on his shoulders. But, strangely enough, Binya crept quietly past the shop, looking the other way, almost as though she was in some way responsible for the misery of Ram Bharosa.

She kept reasoning with herself, telling herself that the umbrella was her very own, and that she couldn't help it if others were jealous of it. But had she loved the umbrella too much? Had it mattered more to her than people mattered? She couldn't help feeling that, in a small way, she was the cause of the sad look on Ram Bharosa's face ('His face is a yard long,' said Bijju) and the ruinous condition of his shop. It was all due to his own greed, no doubt, but she didn't want him to feel too bad about what he'd done, because it made her feel bad about herself; and so she closed the umbrella whenever she came near the shop, opening it again only when she was out of sight.

One day towards the end of October, when she had ten paise in her pocket, she entered the shop and asked the old man for a toffee.

She was Ram Bharosa's first customer in almost two weeks. He looked suspiciously at the girl. Had she come to taunt him, to flaunt the umbrella in his face? She had placed her coin on the counter. Perhaps it was a bad coin. Ram Bharosa picked it up and bit it; he held it up to the light; he rang it on the ground. It was a good coin. He gave Binya the toffee.

Binya had already left the shop when Ram Bharosa saw the closed umbrella lying on his counter. There it was, the blue umbrella he had always wanted, within his grasp at last! He had only to hide it at the back of his shop, and no one would know that he had it, no one could prove that Binya had left it behind.

He stretched out his trembling, bony hand, and took the umbrella by the handle. He pressed it open. He stood beneath it, in the dark shadows of his shop, where no sun or rain could ever touch it.

'But I'm never in the sun or in the rain,' he said aloud. 'Of what use is an umbrella to me?'

And he hurried outside and ran after Binya.

'Binya, Binya!' he shouted. 'Binya, you've left your umbrella behind!'

He wasn't used to running, but he caught up with her, held out the umbrella, saying, 'You forgot it—the umbrella!'

In that moment, it belonged to both of them.

But Binya didn't take the umbrella. She shook her head and said, 'You keep it. I don't need it anymore.'

'But it's such a pretty umbrella!' protested Ram Bharosa. 'It's the best umbrella in the village.'

'I know,' said Binya. 'But an umbrella isn't everything.'

And she left the old man holding the umbrella, and went tripping down the road, and there was nothing between her and the bright blue sky.

VII

Well, now that Ram Bharosa has the blue umbrella—a gift from Binya, as he tells everyone—he is sometimes persuaded to go out into the sun or the rain, and as a result he looks much healthier. Sometimes he uses the umbrella to chase away pigs or goats. It is always left open outside the shop, and anyone who wants to borrow it may do so; and so in a way it has become everyone's umbrella. It is faded and patchy, but it is still the best umbrella in the village.

People are visiting Ram Bharosa's shop again. Whenever Bijju or Binya stop for a cup of tea, he gives them a little extra milk or sugar. They like their tea sweet and milky.

A few nights ago, a bear visited Ram Bharosa's shop. There had been snow on the higher ranges of the Himalayas, and the bear had been finding it difficult to obtain food; so it had come lower down, to see what it could pick up near the village. That night it scrambled on to the tin roof of Ram Bharosa's shop, and made off with a huge pumpkin which had been ripening on the roof. But in climbing off the roof, the bear had lost a claw.

Next morning, Ram Bharosa found the claw just outside the door of his shop. He picked it up and put it in his pocket. A bear's claw was a lucky find.

A day later, when he went into the market town, he took the claw with him, and left it with a silversmith, giving the craftsman certain instructions. The silversmith made a locket for the claw, then he gave it a thin silver chain. When Ram Bharosa came again, he paid the silversmith ten rupees for his work.

The days were growing shorter, and Binya had to be home a little earlier every evening. There was a hungry leopard at large, and she couldn't leave the cows out after dark.

She was hurrying past Ram Bharosa's shop when the old man called out to her.

'Binya, spare a minute! I want to show you something.'

Binya stepped into the shop.

'What do you think of it?' asked Ram Bharosa, showing

her the silver pendant with the claw.

'It's so beautiful,' said Binya, just touching the claw and the silver chain.

'It's a bear's claw,' said Ram Bharosa. 'That's even luckier than a leopard's claw. Would you like to have it?'

'I have no money,' said Binya.

'That doesn't matter. You gave me the umbrella, I give you the claw! Come, let's see what it looks like on you.'

He placed the pendant on Binya, and indeed it looked very beautiful on her.

Ram Bharosa says he will never forget the smile she gave him when she left the shop.

She was halfway home when she realized she had left the cows behind.

'Neelu, Neelu!' she called. 'Oh, Gori!'

There was a faint tinkle of bells as the cows came slowly down the mountain path.

In the distance she could hear her mother and Bijju calling for her.

She began to sing. They heard her singing, and knew she was safe and near.

She walked home through the darkening glade, singing of the stars, and the trees stood still and listened to her, and the mountains were glad.

THE CHERRY TREE

One day, when Rakesh was six, he walked home from the Mussoorie bazaar eating cherries. They were a little sweet, a little sour; small, bright red cherries, which had come all the way from the Kashmir valley.

Here in the Himalayan foothills where Rakesh lived, there were not many fruit trees. The soil was stony, and the dry cold winds stunted the growth of most plants. But on the more sheltered slopes there were forests of oak and deodar.

Rakesh lived with his grandfather on the outskirts of Mussoorie, just where the forest began. His father and mother lived in a small village fifty miles away, where they grew maize and rice and barley in narrow terraced fields on the lower slopes of the mountain. But there were no schools in the village, and Rakesh's parents were keen that he should go to school. As soon as he was of school-going age, they sent him to stay with his grandfather in Mussoorie.

Grandfather was a retired forest ranger. He had a little cottage outside the town.

Rakesh was on his way home from school when he bought the cherries. He paid fifty paise for the bunch. It took him about half-an-hour to walk home, and by the time he reached the cottage, there were only three cherries left.

'Have a cherry, Grandfather,' he said, as soon as he saw his grandfather in the garden.

Grandfather took one cherry and Rakesh promptly ate the other two. He kept the last seed in his mouth for some time, rolling it round and round on his tongue until all the tang had gone. Then he placed the seed on the palm of his hand and studied it.

'Are cherry seeds lucky?' asked Rakesh.

'Of course.'

'Then I'll keep it.'

'Nothing is lucky if you put it away. If you want luck, you must put it to some use.'

'What can I do with a seed?'

'Plant it.'

So Rakesh found a small space and began to dig up a flowerbed.

'Hey, not there,' said Grandfather, 'I've sown mustard in that bed. Plant it in that shady corner, where it won't be disturbed.'

Rakesh went to a corner of the garden where the earth was soft and yielding. He did not have to dig. He pressed the seed into the soil with his thumb and it went right in.

Then he had his lunch, and ran off to play cricket with his friends, and forgot all about the cherry seed.

When it was winter in the hills, a cold wind blew down from the snows and went whoo-whoo-whoo in the deodar trees, and the garden was dry and bare. In the evenings Grandfather and Rakesh sat around a charcoal fire, and Grandfather told Rakesh stories—stories about people who turned into animals, and ghosts who lived in trees, and beans that jumped and stones that wept—and in turn, Rakesh would read to him from the newspaper, Grandfather's eyesight being rather weak. Rakesh found the newspaper very dull—especially after the stories—but Grandfather wanted all the news...

They knew it was spring when the wild duck flew north again, to Siberia. Early in the morning, when he got up to chop wood and light a fire, Rakesh saw the V-shaped formation streaming northward, the calls of the birds carrying clearly through the thin mountain air.

One morning in the garden he bent to pick up what he thought was a small twig and found to his surprise that it was well rooted. He stared at it for a moment, then ran to fetch Grandfather, calling, 'Dada, come and look, the cherry tree has come up!'

'What cherry tree?' asked Grandfather, who had forgotten about it. 'The seed we planted last year—look, it's come up!'

Rakesh went down on his haunches, while Grandfather bent almost double and peered down at the tiny tree. It was about four inches high.

'Yes, it's a cherry tree,' said Grandfather. 'You should water it now and then.'

Rakesh ran indoors and came back with a bucket of water.

'Don't drown it!' said Grandfather.

Rakesh gave it a sprinkling and circled it with pebbles.

'What are the pebbles for?' asked Grandfather.

'For privacy,' said Rakesh.

He looked at the tree every morning but it did not seem to be growing very fast, so he stopped looking at it—except quickly, out of the corner of his eye. And, after a week or two, when he allowed himself to look at it properly, he found that it had grown—at least an inch!

That year the monsoon rains came early and Rakesh plodded to and from school in a raincoat and gum boots. Ferns sprang from the trunks of trees, strange-looking lilies came up in the long grass, and even when it wasn't raining the trees dripped and mist came curling up the valley. The cherry tree grew quickly in this season.

It was about two feet high when a goat entered the garden and ate all the leaves. Only the main stem and two thin branches remained.

'Never mind,' said Grandfather, seeing that Rakesh was upset. 'It will grow again, cherry trees are tough.'

Towards the end of the rainy season new leaves appeared on the tree. Then a woman cutting grass scrambled down the hillside, her scythe swishing through the heavy monsoon foliage. She did not try to avoid the tree—one sweep, and the cherry tree was cut in two.

When Grandfather saw what had happened, he went after the woman and scolded her; but the damage could not be repaired.

'Maybe it will die now,' said Rakesh.

'Maybe,' said Grandfather.

But the cherry tree had no intention of dying.

By the time summer came around again, it had sent out several new shoots with tender green leaves. Rakesh had grown taller too. He was eight now, a sturdy boy with curly black hair and deep black eyes. 'Blackberry eyes,' Grandfather called them.

That monsoon Rakesh went home to his village, to help his father and mother with the planting and ploughing and sowing. He was thinner but stronger when he came back to Grandfather's house at the end of the rains to find that the cherry tree had grown another foot. It was now up to his chest.

Even when there was rain, Rakesh would sometimes water the tree. He wanted it to know that he was there.

One day he found a bright green praying mantis perched on a branch, peering at him with bulging eyes. Rakesh let it remain there; it was the cherry tree's first visitor.

The next visitor was a hairy caterpillar, who started making a meal of the leaves. Rakesh removed it quickly and dropped it on a heap of dry leaves.

'Come back when you're a butterfly,' he said.

Winter came early. The cherry tree bent low with the weight of snow. Field mice sought shelter in the roof of the cottage. The road from the valley was blocked, and for several days there was no newspaper, and this made Grandfather quite grumpy. His stories began to have unhappy endings.

In February it was Rakesh's birthday. He was nine—and the tree was four, but almost as tall as Rakesh.

One morning, when the sun came out, Grandfather came into the garden, 'to let some warmth get into my bones,' as he put it. He stopped in front of the cherry tree, stared at it for a few moments, and then called out, 'Rakesh! Come and look! Come quickly before it falls!'

Rakesh and Grandfather gazed at the tree as though it had performed a miracle. There was a pale pink blossom at the end of a branch.

The following year there were more blossoms. And suddenly the tree was taller than Rakesh, even though it was less than half his age. And then it was taller than Grandfather, who was older than some of the oak trees.

But Rakesh had grown too. He could run and jump and climb trees as well as most boys, and he read a lot of books, although he still liked listening to Grandfather's tales.

In the cherry tree, bees came to feed on the nectar in the blossoms, and tiny birds pecked at the blossoms and broke them off. But the tree kept blossoming right through the spring, and there were always more blossoms than birds.

That summer there were small cherries on the tree. Rakesh tasted one and spat it out.

'It's too sour,' he said.

They'll be better next year,' said Grandfather.

But the birds liked them—especially the bigger birds, such as the bulbuls and scarlet minivets—and they flitted in and out of the foliage, feasting on the cherries.

On a warm sunny afternoon, when even the bees looked sleepy, Rakesh was looking for Grandfather without finding him in any of his favourite places around the house. Then he looked out of the bedroom window and saw Grandfather reclining on a cane chair under the cherry tree.

There's just the right amount of shade here,' said Grandfather. 'And I like looking at the leaves.'

They're pretty leaves,' said Rakesh. 'And they are always ready to dance, if there's a breeze.'

After Grandfather had come indoors, Rakesh went into the garden and lay down on the grass beneath the tree. He gazed up through the leaves at the great blue sky; and turning on his side, he could see the mountains striding away into the clouds. He was still lying beneath the tree when the evening shadows crept across the garden. Grandfather came back and sat down beside Rakesh, and they waited in silence until the stars came out and the nightjar began to call. In the forest below, the crickets and cicadas began tuning up; and suddenly the trees were full of the sound of insects.

'There are so many trees in the forest,' said Rakesh, What's so special about this tree? Why do we like it so much?'

'We planted it ourselves,' said Grandfather. That's why it's special.'

'Just one small seed,' said Rakesh, and he touched the smooth bark of the tree that he had grown. He ran his hand along the trunk of the tree and put his finger to the tip of a leaf. 'I wonder,' he whispered. 'Is this what it feels to be God?'

SUSANNA'S SEVEN HUSBANDS

Locally the tomb was known as 'the grave of the seven times married one'.

You'd be forgiven for thinking it was Bluebeard's grave; he was reputed to have killed several wives in turn because they showed undue curiosity about a locked room. But this was the tomb of Susanna Anna-Maria Yeates, and the inscription (most of it in Latin) stated that she was mourned by all who had benefitted from her generosity, her beneficiaries having included various schools, orphanages and the church across the road. There was no sign of any other grave in the vicinity and presumably her husbands had been interred in the old Rajpur graveyard, below the Delhi Ridge.

I was still in my teens when I first saw the ruins of what had once been a spacious and handsome mansion. Desolate and silent, its well-laid paths were overgrown with weeds, and its flower beds had disappeared under a growth of thorny jungle. The two-storeyed house had looked across the Grand Trunk Road. Now abandoned, feared and shunned, it stood encircled in mystery, reputedly the home of evil spirits.

Outside the gate, along the Grand Trunk Road, thousands of

vehicles sped by—cars, trucks, buses, tractors, bullock carts—but few noticed the old mansion or its mausoleum, set back as they were from the main road, hidden by mango, neem and peepul trees. One old and massive peepul tree grew out of the ruins of the house, strangling it much as its owner was said to have strangled one of her dispensable paramours.

As a much-married person with a quaint habit of disposing of her husbands whenever she tired of them, Susanna's malignant spirit was said to haunt the deserted garden. I had examined the tomb, I had gazed upon the ruins, I had scrambled through shrubbery and overgrown rose bushes, but I had not encountered the spirit of this mysterious woman. Perhaps, at the time, I was too pure and innocent to be targeted by malignant spirits. For malignant she must have been, if the stories about her were true.

The vaults of the ruined mansion were rumoured to contain a buried treasure—the amassed wealth of the lady Susanna. But no one dared go down there, for the vaults were said to be occupied by a family of cobras, traditional guardians of buried treasure. Had she really been a woman of great wealth, and could treasure still be buried there? I put these questions to Naushad, the furniture-maker, who had lived in the vicinity all his life, and whose father had made the furniture and fittings for this and other great houses in Old Delhi.

'Lady Susanna, as she was known, was much sought after for her wealth,' recalled Naushad. 'She was no miser, either. She spent freely, reigning in state in her palatial home, with many horses and carriages at her disposal. Every evening she rode through the Roshanara Gardens, the cynosure of all eyes, for she was beautiful as well as wealthy. Yes, all men sought her favours, and she could choose from the best of them. Many were fortune hunters. She did not discourage them. Some found favour for a time, but she soon tired of them. None of her husbands enjoyed her wealth for very long!

'Today no one enters those ruins, where once there was mirth and laughter. She was a zamindari lady, the owner of much land, and she administered her estate with a strong hand. She was kind if rents were paid when they fell due, but terrible if someone failed to pay.

'Well, over fifty years have gone by since she was laid to rest, but still men speak of her with awe. Her spirit is restless, and it is said that she often visits the scenes of her former splendour. She has been seen walking through this gate, or riding in the gardens, or driving in her phaeton down the Rajpur road.'

'And what happened to all those husbands?' I asked.

'Most of them died mysterious deaths. Even the doctors were baffled. Tomkins sahib drank too much. The lady soon tired of him. A drunken husband is a burdensome creature, she was heard to say. He would eventually have drunk himself to death, but she was an impatient woman and was anxious to replace him. You see those datura bushes growing wild in the grounds? They have always done well here.'

'Belladonna?' I suggested.

'That's right, huzoor. Introduced in the whisky soda, it put him to sleep forever.'

'She was quite humane in her way.'

'Oh, very humane, sir. She hated to see anyone suffer. One sahib, I don't know his name, drowned in the tank behind the house, where the water lilies grew. But she made sure he was half dead before he fell in. She had large, powerful hands, they said.'

'Why did she bother to marry them? Couldn't she just have had men friends?'

'Not in those days, huzoor. Respectable society would not

have tolerated it. Neither in India nor in the West would it have been permitted.'

'She was born out of her time,' I remarked.

'True, sir. And remember, most of them were fortune hunters. So we need not waste too much pity on them.'

'She did not waste any.'

'She was without pity. Especially when she found out what they were really after. Snakes had a better chance of survival.'

'How did the other husbands take their leave of this world?'

'Well, the Colonel sahib shot himself while cleaning his rifle. Purely an accident, huzoor. Although some say she had loaded his gun without his knowledge. Such was her reputation by now that she was suspected even when innocent. But she bought her way out of trouble. It was easy enough if you were wealthy.'

'And the fourth husband?'

'Oh, he died a natural death. There was a cholera epidemic that year, and he was carried off by the haija. Although, again, there were some who said that a good dose of arsenic produced the same symptoms! Anyway, it was cholera on the death certificate. And the doctor who signed it was the next to marry her.'

'Being a doctor, he was probably quite careful about what he ate and drank.'

'He lasted about a year.'

'What happened?'

'He was bitten by a cobra.'

'Well, that was just bad luck, wasn't it? You could hardly blame it on Susanna.'

'No, huzoor, but the cobra was in his bedroom. It was coiled around the bedpost. And when he undressed for the night, it struck! He was dead when Susanna came into the room an hour later. She had a way with snakes. She did not harm them and they never attacked her.'

'And there were no antidotes in those days. Exit the doctor. Who was the sixth husband?'

'A handsome man. An indigo planter. He had gone bankrupt when the indigo trade came to an end. He was hoping to recover his fortune with the good lady's help. But our Susanna mem, she did not believe in sharing her fortune with anyone.'

'How did she remove the indigo planter?'

'It was said that she lavished strong drink upon him, and when he lay helpless, she assisted him on the road we all have to take by pouring molten lead in his ears.'

'A painless death, I'm told.'

'But a terrible price to pay, huzoor, simply because one is no longer needed...'

We walked along the dusty highway, enjoying the evening breeze, and sometime later we entered the Roshanara Gardens, in those days Delhi's most popular and fashionable meeting place.

'You have told me how six of her husbands died, Naushad. I thought there were seven?'

'Ah, the seventh was a gallant young magistrate who perished right here, huzoor. They were driving through the park after dark when the lady's carriage was attacked by brigands. In defending her, the young man received a fatal sword wound.'

'Not the lady's fault, Naushad.'

'No, huzoor. But he was a magistrate, remember, and the assailants, one of whose relatives had been convicted by him, were out for revenge. Oddly enough, though, two of the men were given employment by the lady Susanna at a later date. You may draw your own conclusions.'

'And were there others?'

'Not husbands. But an adventurer, a soldier of fortune came

along. He found her treasure, they say. And he lies buried with it, in the cellars of the ruined house. His bones lie scattered there, among gold and silver and precious jewels. The cobras guard them still! But how he perished was a mystery, and remains so till this day.'

'And Susanna? What happened to her?'

'She lived to a ripe old age. If she paid for her crimes, it wasn't in this life! She had no children, but she started an orphanage and gave generously to the poor and to various schools and institutions, including a home for widows. She died peacefully in her sleep.'

'A merry widow,' I remarked. 'The Black Widow spider!'

Don't go looking for Susanna's tomb. It vanished some years ago, along with the ruins of her mansion. A smart new housing estate has come up on the site, but not before several workmen and a contractor succumbed to snakebite! Occasionally, residents complain of a malignant ghost in their midst, who is given to flagging down cars, especially those driven by single men. There have also been one or two mysterious disappearances.

And after dusk, an old-fashioned horse and carriage can sometimes be seen driving through the Roshanara Gardens. If you chance upon it, ignore it, my friend. Don't stop to answer any questions from the beautiful fair lady who smiles at you from behind lace curtains. She's still looking for her final victim.

HASSAN, THE BAKER*

I needed somewhere to stay, if I was going to spend some time in Fosterganj.

Melaram directed me to the local bakery. Hassan, the baker, had a room above his shop that had lain vacant since he built it a few years ago. An affable man, Hassan was the proud father of a dozen children; I say dozen at random, because I never did get to ascertain the exact number as they were never in one place at the same time. They did not live in the room above the bakery, which was much too small, but in a rambling old building below the bazaar, which housed a number of large families—the baker's, the tailor's, the postman's, among others.

I was shown the room. It was scantily furnished, the bed taking up almost half the space. A small table and chair stood near the window. Windows are important. I find it impossible to live in a room without a window. This one provided a view of the street and the buildings on the other side. Nothing very inspiring, but at least it wouldn't be dull.

A narrow bathroom was attached to the room. Hassan

---

*From *Tales of Fosterganj*

was very proud of it, because he had recently installed a flush tank and western-style potty. I complimented him on the potty and said it looked very comfortable. But what really took my fancy was the bathroom window. It hadn't been opened for some time, and the glass panes were caked with dirt. But when finally we got it open, the view was remarkable. Below the window was a sheer drop of two or three hundred feet. Ahead, an open vista, a wide valley, and then the mountains striding away towards the horizon. I don't think any hotel in town had such a splendid view. I could see myself sitting for hours on that potty, enraptured, enchanted, having the valley and the mountains all to myself. Almost certain constipation of course, but I would take that risk.

'Forty rupees a month,' said Hassan, and I gave him two months' rent on the spot.

'I'll move in next week,' I said. 'First I have to bring my books from Delhi.'

On my way back to the town I took a shortcut through the forest. A swarm of yellow butterflies drifted across the path. A woodpecker pecked industriously on the bark of a tree, searching for young cicadas. Overhead, wild duck flew north, on their way across Central Asia, all travelling without passports. Birds and butterflies recognize no borders.

I hadn't been this way before, and I was soon lost. Two village boys returning from town with their milk cans gave me the wrong directions. I was put on the right path by a girl who was guiding a cow home. There was something about her fresh face and bright smile that I found tremendously appealing. She was less than beautiful but more than pretty, if you know what I mean. A face to remember.

A little later I found myself in an open clearing, with a large pool in the middle. Its still waters looked very deep. At one end there were steps, apparently for bathers. But the water did not look very inviting. It was a sunless place, several old oaks shutting out the light. Fallen off leaves floated on the surface. No birds sang. It was a strange, haunted sort of place. I hurried on...

It did not take me long to settle down in my little room above the bakery. Recent showers had brought out the sheen on new leaves, transformed the grass on the hillside from a faded yellow to an emerald green. A barbet atop a spruce tree was in full cry. It would keep up its monotonous chant all summer. And early morning, a whistling-thrush would render its interrupted melody, never quite finishing what it had to say.

It was good to hear the birds and laughing schoolchildren through my open window. But I soon learnt to shut it whenever I went out. Late one morning, on returning from my walk, I found a large rhesus monkey sitting on my bed, tearing up a loaf of bread that Hassan had baked for me. I tried to drive the fellow away, but he seemed reluctant to leave. He bared his teeth and swore at me in monkey language. Then he stuffed a piece of bread into his mouth and glared at me, daring me to do my worst. I recalled that monkeys carry rabies, and not wanting to join those who had recently been bitten by rabid dogs, I backed out of the room and called for help. One of Hassan's brood came running up the steps with a hockey stick, and chased the invader away.

'Always keep a mug of water handy,' he told me. 'Throw the water on him and he'll be off. They hate cold water.'

'You may be right,' I said. 'I've never seen a monkey taking a bath.'

'See how miserable they are when it rains,' said my rescuer. 'They huddle together as though it's the end of the world.'

'Strange, isn't it? Birds like bathing in the rain.'

'So do I. Wait till the monsoon comes. You can join me then.'
'Perhaps I will.'

On this friendly note we parted, and I cleaned up the mess made by my simian visitor, and then settled down to do some writing.

But there was something about the atmosphere of Fosterganj that discouraged any kind of serious work or effort. Tucked away in a fold of the hills, its inhabitants had begun to resemble their surroundings: one old man resembled a willow bent by rain and wind; an elderly lady with her umbrella reminded me of a colourful mushroom, quite possibly poisonous; my good baker-cum-landlord looked like a bit of the hillside, scarred and uneven but stable. The children were like young grass, coming up all over the place; but the adolescents were like nettles, you never knew if they would sting when touched. There was a young Tibetan lady whose smile was like the blue sky opening up. And there was no brighter blue than the sky as seen from Fosterganj on a clear day.

It took me some time to get to know all the inhabitants. But one of the first was Professor Lulla, recently retired, who came hurrying down the road like the White Rabbit in *Alice in Wonderland*, glancing at his watch and muttering to himself. If, like the White Rabbit, he was saying 'I'm late, I'm late!' I wouldn't have been at all surprised. I was standing outside the bakery, chatting to one of the children, when he came up to me, adjusted his spectacles, peered at me through murky lenses, and said, 'Welcome to Fosterganj, sir. I believe you've come to stay for the season.'

'I'm not sure how long I'll stay,' I said. 'But thank you for your welcome.'

'We must get together and have a cultural and cultured exchange,' he said, rather pompously. 'Not many intellectuals in Fosterganj, you know.'

'I was hoping there wouldn't be.'

'But we'll talk, we'll talk. Only can't stop now. I have a funeral to attend. Eleven o'clock at the Camel's Back cemetery. Poor woman. Dead. Quite dead. Would you care to join me?'

'Er—I'm not in the party mood,' I said. 'And I don't think I knew the deceased.'

'Old Miss Gamleh. Your landlord thought she was a flowerpot—would have been ninety next month. Wonderful woman. Hated chokra-boys.' He looked distastefully at the boy grinning up at him. 'Stole all her plums, if the monkeys didn't get them first. Spent all her life in the hill station. Never married. Jilted by a weedy British colonel, awful fellow, even made off with her savings. But she managed on her own. Kept poultry, sold eggs to the hotels.'

'What happens to the poultry?' I asked.

'Oh, hens can look after themselves,' he said airily. 'But I can't linger or I'll be late. It's a long walk to the cemetery.'

And he set off in determined fashion, like Scott of the Antarctic about to brave a blizzard.

'Must have been a close friend, the old lady who passed away,' I remarked.

'Not at all,' said Hassan, who had been standing in his doorway listening to the conversation. 'I doubt if she ever spoke to him. But Professor Lulla never misses a funeral. He goes to all of them—cremations, burials—funerals of any well-known person, even strangers. It's a hobby with him.'

'Extraordinary,' I said. 'I thought collecting match-box labels was sad enough as a hobby. Doesn't it depress him?'

'It seems to cheer him up, actually. But I must go too, sir. If you don't mind keeping an eye on the bakery for an hour or two, I'll hurry along to the funeral and see if I can get her poultry cheap. Miss Gamleh's hens give good eggs, I'm told. Little Ali will look after the customers, sir. All you have to do is see that they don't make off with the buns and cream-rolls.'

I don't know if Hassan attended the funeral, but he came back with two baskets filled with cackling hens, and a rooster to keep them company.

GRACIE[*]

> Show me the way to go home,
> I'm tired and I want to go to bed,
> I had a little drink but an hour ago,
> And it's gone right to my head...

A group of British soldiers, a little drunk, were singing in the middle of the road. It was almost midnight. And yes, it was World War II. But it wasn't a street in Paris or Naples or Rangoon—it was Rajpur Road in Dehradun, then a small town tucked away in the Doon Valley some 200 miles north of New Delhi.

The soldiers were on leave. Not home leave, because they were still far from home—but a break from active duty on the warfront, from the fighting in Burma and the Far East. Dehradun had been designated a 'recreational centre' for Allied troops. Unfortunately, we in Dehra could provide little by way of recreation for these restless young men, who were looking for something more than food and drink.

---

[*]From *Secrets*

Coming down the street from the other end of town were a group of American soldiers. They too were engaged in a sing-song. 'Sweet Rosie O'Grady' or something very Irish. They had more money to throw around, as they were better paid than the British soldiers. There was no love lost between these 'allies'. Someone made an insulting gesture and remark, and soon there was a brawl in the middle of the road.

Looking down at them from the balcony of our flat above the road, I asked my mother: 'Has World War III begun?'

'It looks like it,' she said.

'Who's winning?'

A couple of soldiers were already flat on the ground.

'The military police. Here they come!'

A jeep-load of military police, British and American, drove up, and showed their solidarity in the midst of hostilities by rounding up the drunken brigade and carrying them off to barracks.

Silence descended on Rajpur Road, and I went back to bed.

◆

It was the winter of 1944–45, a few months after I'd lost my father, and I was back in Dehra for the winter holidays. My mother and stepfather were always moving from one house or flat to another (usually under pressure from the landlord), and that year we had a flat in Astley Hall, right in the centre of town.

Astley Hall and its environs were having something of a boom during the war years, due mainly to the presence of several thousand Allied troops stationed outside Dehradun. Casinos, cafes and dance halls had sprung up in this otherwise sedate centre of town, and every evening they would be filled to capacity with rowdy roistering soldiers who had survived the fighting but who might well have to return to active duty before long.

To avoid bar fights and street brawls, the Americans were allowed into town three days a week, the British three days a week, and the Italian prisoners of war once a week.

The Italians were the best behaved. They were, after all, war prisoners and confined to a prison camp six days in the week. Nor did they have money to throw around, so they made a little pocket money by selling postage stamps and handmade toys.

The American soldiers had unlimited supplies of chewing gum, and these they distributed freely amongst the children of the locality. Naturally this made them the most popular of the visiting soldiers.

The British did not have much to offer by way of surplus rations, but one young corporal, more educated than his fellows, gave me three well-thumbed paperbacks in the Collins Crime Club Series, and through them I made my first acquaintance with the works of Agatha Christie, Edgar Wallace, and Peter Cheyney. As a result I became a lifelong addict of the crime novel.

This same young corporal took more than a casual interest in one of our neighbours, a girl called Gracie, who lived in the next flat with her elder sister, a schoolteacher. Gracie was just seventeen or eighteen, a very pretty girl of mixed English, Portuguese, Burmese and Indian descent. A terrific combination of genes and hereditary traits. And physically she had inherited the best of all worlds. No one could have been lovelier. Coffee-coloured, sloe-eyed, with glossy black hair and full inviting lips, she had only to walk down the street for heads to turn in her direction. At ten, I was madly in love with her.

Gracie had a good singing voice—sweet and low and a little husky—and she had been engaged by bandmaster Billy Cotton to sing a few numbers during the late evening dances and cabaret shows at the Casino, Dehra's very own 'nightclub'. We had never had a nightclub before the war, and as far as I know there hasn't been one after Independence—not yet, anyway. But in those jolly wartime years, with everyone panting for a little pleasure, the Casino provided music, dance, food and drink, and a 'magic show'.

For the Casino was owned by 'Mustafa Pasha' (real name Roshan Kapoor), one of the country's foremost conjurers and magicians.

Every evening, for an hour, he'd put on a magic show, doing card tricks, taking rabbits out of hats, paper streamers out of his mouth, and eggs out of his customers' pockets. He climaxed it by sawing his teenaged daughter in half. She was none the worse for it, naturally.

When the magic show was over, the singing and dancing commenced, and so did the boozing. By midnight the place was in an uproar, chairs flying about, tables overturned, one or two soldiers flat on their backs—knocked out by drink or one of their comrades. The enemy would have loved it.

Gracie would evade the last lurching warrior, slip out from beneath his grasping arms, and leave the Casino by the back entrance. One of the cooks, a local boy, would escort her home.

Gracie received two hundred rupees a month for singing to the troops, which was what her sister got for teaching little children to read and write. Gracie sang at a nightclub, her sister (I forget her name) taught at a convent. And yet, Gracie was the brighter of the two. She had more conversation, more wit, more joie de vivre.

And we had one thing in common—we both enjoyed chaat.

Every evening a chaat wallah would come around to the Astley Hall shops and flats, preparing chaat on the spot. Served on large green leaves, the chaat and kachalu, flavoured with lemon juice, tamarind juice, chillies and garam masala, was almost an addiction. I did not always have enough pocket money, cheap though it was, but Gracie would call me over and make sure I had as much chaat as I could consume. Corporal Allen did not approve of the chaat, but would occasionally give me a rupee and tell me to run off and buy toffees, so that he could have Gracie to himself for ten or fifteen minutes. I did not care for toffees, but I would keep the rupee and come back after five minutes to find them kissing on the veranda.

The corporal was a little too refined for the Casino, and contented himself with taking Gracie to the pictures. We had three cinemas showing English or American films—the Orient, the Odeon, and the Hollywood. Once Gracie took me to the pictures—it was a sentimental drama called *Always in My Heart*—and we held hands throughout the show. I had got the better of Corporal Allen that day.

At the Casino, Gracie sang sentimental ballads such as 'Smoke Gets in Your Eyes' and 'White Christmas', and although Dehra did not get a white Christmas, we got a white New Year on the evening of 31 December.

My mother was in bed, having that week given birth to my baby brother. I was knocking a football around on the parade ground with Bhim and Ranbir and some of the local boys when, to everyone's delight and consternation, it began to snow. As far as we knew it had never snowed in Dehra, so it was a unique, almost freakish event. We ran about, shouting in excitement while it continued snowing, so that by late evening the town was covered with a glistening white mantle. I ran home, breathless with excitement, and told my mother it was snowing outside.

'Don't try to make a fool of me,' she said 'I'm not in the mood for your silly jokes.'

So I went outside and broke off a branch of the litchi tree. The leaves were covered with snow. I took indoors and showed it to my mother, and she said, 'the last time it snowed here was around forty years ago—1905, the year your grandparents were married. It was snowing outside St Thomas's church just as they were taking their marriage vows.'

'They must have seen it as a good sign,' I said.

'Well, they were married for thirty years until your grandfather died.'

'And they had lots of children.'

'Five girls and one spoilt brat of a boy—your Uncle Ken. But I was the youngest and they spoilt me too.'

♦

That night, New Year's Eve, there was a grand dance at the Casino, and Gracie persuaded my mother to allow me to go along with her. I was to sit in a corner of the dance hall and avoid fraternizing with the partying soldiers.

It was an eventful evening. The snowfall had made New Year's Eve even more special, and the dance hall was crowded, mostly with high-spirited soldiers, but there were also a few of the local gentry and their families.

Mustafa Pasha, uttering magical incantations, went through his usual routine, which was always popular—and this was followed by three or four sentimental ballads sung by Gracie to the accompaniment of Billy Cotton's four-piece band. Gracie wasn't a great singer, but her freshness, energy and sensuality always brought the house down—as it did that New Year's Eve.

I had a small table to myself in a corner of the dance hall, and Gracie saw to it that I was well supplied with my favourite fish fingers, chips, gulab jamuns, and Vimto—the last, a raspberry-flavoured soft drink that was very popular during the war years. Whatever happened to Vimto? Killed off, no doubt, by all the colas and fizzy drinks that came in later.

Between songs, Gracie would come over to see if I was all

right. I must have been the only boy in a roomful of adults. The soldiers whistled and called to Gracie to come over to their table for a change, but she simply smiled good-naturedly and went back to the rostrum to give a fair imitation of Lena Horne. She had the same sultry presence as the famous blues singer.

At midnight the lights went out and everyone began to sing 'Auld Lang Syne'.

> Should old acquaintance be forgot
> And never brought to mind?...
> We'll drink a cup of kindness yet,
> For auld lang syne...

Gracie was standing beside me, singing, and I stood up and took her hand. I loved listening to her singing. My own voice was ragged and tuneless and I thought it best not to inflict it on others.

'Come, Ruskin, give me a kiss,' said Gracie, leaning over me, and I suddenly found my lips pressed against hers in what was, till then, the most magical moment of my life. It was the first time I'd been kissed full on the lips, and I wanted that kiss to go on forever.

But the lights came on, and we drew apart, and everyone shouted 'HAPPY NEW YEAR!' The band struck up again and Gracie sang 'The White Cliffs of Dover', which made the British soldiers very maudlin and homesick.

At two in the morning I accompanied Gracie back to our adjoining flats, but there were no further kisses, as by then we had been joined by Corporal Allen who had missed the party but had turned up to escort us home. I found myself fervently wishing that he'd be sent back to Burma or wherever the fighting was going on.

♦

I have to admit that Gracie did not see me in the same romantic light that I saw her. She looked upon me as a younger brother, and treated me with the openness and light-hearted affection that she would have bestowed on a brother, had there been one.

'Press my back, will you, Ruskin?' she pleaded more than once. 'I can hardly stand straight.'

Most willingly did I oblige, knowing full well that I would not have been assigned this delicious task had I been an adult. I might well have grown up to be a physiotherapist had my holidays not come to an end.

On more than one occasion Gracie changed her dress in front of me, and I saw her lovely breasts and supple waist and thighs as she studied herself in the mirror, almost oblivious of my presence.

I noticed a long scar on her lower abdomen and asked her how she'd got it.

'Oh, when I was in school up in Mussoorie,' she said. 'Dr Butcher removed my appendix.'

'Dr Butcher! Was he a butcher or a doctor?'

'He was the civil surgeon. And he had a thing about appendixes. If you went to him with a tummy ache, he cut you open and took out your appendix. He said it was at the root of all our problems! He had so much difficulty finding mine that he had to make an extra-large cut.'

'Can I touch it?'

'Of course. It doesn't hurt now.'

I ran my finger along her scar. I found it quite thrilling to be touching her like that.

'You don't have to stop at the scar,' said Gracie with a laugh. 'You can touch other places too.'

But I was too shy to be making further explorations. For a ten-year-old, the scar was more fascinating than her hips or her navel. But it put me on terms of close familiarity. Even Corporal Allen hadn't seen her scar, or so she assured me!

♦

My boarding school was in Simla, a day and a night's train journey from Dehra, so when my three-month-long winter holidays were over and I returned to school, I knew it would be nine long months before I came home to Dehra.

In that time a lot could happen, and it generally did. For one thing, the war ended and all the soldiers went home—to England or America or wherever they'd come from. A few war brides went with them. A few illegitimate children were left behind in various countries. Also, everyone knew that India's independence was just around the corner, and the Anglo-Indians and the 'country-born' British were beginning to pack their bags.

When I came home to Dehra in the winter of 1945–46, the Casino, the dance hall and cafes had vanished, and the town was going through something of a slump.

'Where's Gracie?' I asked my mother, as soon as I was home.

'Gracie's in England. She married that baby-faced corporal who used to hang around her all the time. But her sister's still here, teaching at the convent. Do you want some help with your maths?'

'No.' There was nothing romantic about maths.

Mustafa Pasha was missing too. He had moved to Bombay, where he was making a fortune.

I can't say I missed anyone very much. At eleven, I had my priorities, and they were the four Cs—the cinemas, comics, chaat and Crime Club thrillers, all in that order. With the exception of the chaat, I had, till then, absorbed very little of Indian culture. It was the same with most Anglo-Indian boys of my age. They went to hill schools and came home to railway colonies and

Saturday night dance parties. Some of them excelled at hockey and made it to the Olympics. I played football and occasionally cricket, and the boys I played with were the children of Indian shopkeepers or clerks—boys who, when they grew up, would be the backbone of the prosperous middle class.

Sometimes I accompanied Bhim or Ranbir to a Hindi movie, but most of the time I haunted English cinemas which were still running, although to smaller audiences.

Dehra–Simla, Simla–Dehra, and the years slipped by, and before I knew it I was a young man just out of school and without any prospects. I suppose I could have gone to the local college, or joined the army (the truly Indian Army, the British having left three years previously), or possibly got a job on a tea estate; but none of these prospects thrilled me. I wanted to be a happy writer, even though readers were in short supply in 1950s India.

Sensibly, my mother packed me off to the UK. I had to take a job there, of course. There was no one to see me through a college or university. Even the Regent Street polytechnic was beyond my means. In any case, I was not interested in acquiring a degree. Any kind of work would do, provided I could sit down in my bedsitter over the weekends, sometimes at night, and work on the novel that I had resolved to finish.

For three months I worked in a grocery store, then moved up in the social hierarchy by taking a job as an accounts clerk in a firm making photographic goods and accessories. It was boring work—simple arithmetic, really—but it allowed my mind to wander in various other directions. And the pay packet, a basic wage of five pounds a week, covered my living expenses.

It was a lonely life. Every evening I would return to my cold and silent room, turn on the gas, make myself a Marmite sandwich, and sit down to work on my literary opus.

Just occasionally I would go to a cinema or theatre, or take a meal in a cheap restaurant. Sometimes, late at night, I would walk about the city—London's streets were comparatively safe in those days, although occasionally there were gang fights and hold-ups.

The prostitutes would stand, as they always did, every ten yards down the left-hand side of the road, keeping to fixed pitches for the sale of their overripe wares. It was difficult to find one who was under thirty.

Whenever I came out of a cinema in the Piccadilly area, I would walk past them, feigning indifference; but I would steal covert glances at these women, hoping to see someone young and pretty. At eighteen, I was anxious to lose my virginity and prove my manhood. At eighteen, time seems to be passing very swiftly. Any day, I used to think, I shall be old, too old for love, too old for sex, too old for an affair. Young men in the office spoke of their dalliance with flirtatious girls, of sexual adventures in their teens. I had nothing to boast about. I was still an innocent—untried as a lover—and I felt that this was something that had to be remedied.

Late one evening, as I passed a young woman who was a little different from the others—sultry-looking, with Asiatic features—I stopped and looked back, and she smiled and gave me the usual line: 'Come along, darling, I'll give you a good time.' And summoning up a little courage, I went along, hoping for a good time the first time.

She took me down a side street, to a seedy-looking lodging house, and up some stairs to her room—where, without ado, she thrust a large biscuit tin at me. Only it didn't contain biscuits, it held condoms.

'You'd better use one,' she said.

Not the most romantic way to get going, but she was

obviously in a hurry—other customers were waiting!

I tried fondling her, stroking her breasts, but she said there wasn't time for all that. She pulled up her dress. She had varicose veins—probably from too much street-walking. She pulled down her knickers, and that was when I saw the scar.

I could not have mistaken the scar—Dr Butcher's over-eager attempt to locate an appendix.

'Gracie?' I stammered.

She looked hard at me then, and recognition flooded her painted face. Under the heavy make-up, it was Gracie. And I was no longer a ten-year-old. I was an awkward young man trying to prove his manhood.

Desire had died in me the minute I recognized the girl I used to know; all the freshness and romance and youth had vanished, leaving her a well-paid chattel for the gratification of lonely, loveless men.

And all I could say was, 'What happened to Corporal Allen?'

Well, it appeared that Corporal Allen had ditched Gracie soon after they had arrived in Britain. He had been posted in West Berlin, where he had taken up with a fräulein. Gracie had tried to put her talents as a singer to good use, but torch singers were cheaper by the dozen, and she was unable to break into show business. She spent a year working in a garment factory on a basic wage. An engaging young pimp had persuaded her and a couple of other attractive girls to join a West End brothel, and there she was now, still fighting fit although a little battle worn. But she had saved some money.

'In a year or two I'll retire from this racket and start a little boarding house near the sea. Down on the south coast. It's warmer there. I do miss India, though. How's my sister?'

'She's fine. Might start her own school soon. Don't you write to her?'

'Will do, one of these days.'

I got up to leave. I might have had a crush on Gracie when I was a boy, but I couldn't possibly make love to her now. It would be like having sex with a close relative.

'You don't have to go,' she said. 'We can sit and talk.'

'You must have other engagements.'

'No,' she said. 'As soon as you've gone I'll be out on the streets again, trying to hook someone.'

'You're a good hooker. You hooked me all right.'

She laughed then. And her laughter was still the same—unforced, genuine. Some things don't change.

'Is this your first time, then?'

I nodded. 'You were the only girl on the street who had any appeal for me. Perhaps, subconsciously, I recognized you. But it was only when I saw that old scar of yours that I *knew*...'

'And now?'

'No, not now. I couldn't.'

'But you'll come again?'

'We'll meet again.'

There was a loud knocking on the door.

'My landlady,' said Gracie, and went to the door. A formidable-looking madam was waiting outside.

'You've been a long time, dearie.' She looked me up and down. 'Just out of school, too, by the looks of him.'

'He's just leaving.'

'And there's a gentleman in my parlour who's asking for you. Seems he took a fancy to you the last time he was here. Oldish, but well-heeled.'

'I'll be down in a jiffy.'

Gracie gave me a hug and kissed me on the cheek. As I stepped into the street, the strains of an old song floated after me. It came from someone's record-player in one of the apartments. Vera Lynn. But it might have been Gracie...

> We'll meet again,
> Don't know where
> Don't know when,
> But we'll meet again,
> Some sunny day...

We never met again. Life took me in another direction. It usually does. But I hope Gracie saved enough to start a little boarding house in some sunny seaside resort. She deserved something better than a brothel.

DINNER WITH FOSTER*

Straddling a spur of the Mussoorie range as it dips into the Doon valley, Fosterganj came into existence some two hundred years ago and was almost immediately forgotten. And today it is not very different from what it was in 1961, when I lived there briefly.

A quiet corner, where I could live like a recluse and write my stories—that was what I was looking for. And in Fosterganj I thought I'd found my retreat: a cluster of modest cottages, a straggling little bazaar, a post office, a crumbling castle (supposedly haunted), a mountain stream at the bottom of the hill, a winding footpath that took you either uphill or down. What more could one ask for? It reminded me a little of an English village, and indeed that was what it had once been; a tiny settlement on the outskirts of the larger hill station. But the British had long since gone, and the residents were now a fairly mixed lot.

I forget what took me to Fosterganj in the first place. Destiny, perhaps; although I'm not sure why destiny would have bothered

---

*From *Tales of Fosterganj*

to guide an itinerant writer to an obscure hamlet in the hills. Chance would be a better word. For chance plays a great part in all our lives. And it was just by chance that I found myself in the Fosterganj bazaar one fine morning early in May. The oaks and maples were in new leaf; geraniums flourished on sunny balconies; a boy delivering milk whistled a catchy Dev Anand song; a mule train clattered down the street. The chill of winter had gone and there was warmth in the sunshine that played upon old walls.

I sat in a tea shop, tested my teeth on an old bun, and washed it down with milky tea. The bun had been around for some time, but so had I, so we were quits. At the age of forty I could digest almost anything.

The tea shop owner, Melaram, was a friendly sort, as are most tea shop owners. He told me that not many tourists made their way down to Fosterganj. The only attraction was the waterfall, and you had to be fairly fit in order to scramble down the steep and narrow path that led to the ravine where a little stream came tumbling over the rocks. I would visit it one day, I told him.

'Then you should stay here a day or two,' said Melaram. 'Explore the stream. Walk down to Rajpur. You'll need a good walking stick. Look, I have several in my shop. Cherry wood, walnut wood, oak.' He saw me wavering. 'You'll also need one to climb the next hill—it's called Pari Tibba.' I was charmed by the name—Fairy Hill.

I hadn't planned on doing much walking that day—the walk down to Fosterganj from Mussoorie had already taken almost an hour—but I liked the look of a sturdy cherry-wood walking stick, and I bought one for two rupees. Those were the days of simple living. You don't see two-rupee notes anymore. You don't see walking sticks either. Hardly anyone walks.

I strolled down the small bazaar, without having to worry about passing cars and lorries or a crush of people. Two or three schoolchildren were sauntering home, burdened by their school bags bursting with homework. A cow and a couple of stray dogs examined the contents of an overflowing dustbin. A policeman sitting on a stool outside a tiny police outpost yawned, stretched, stood up, looked up and down the street in anticipation of crimes to come, scratched himself in the anal region and sank back upon his stool.

A man in a crumpled shirt and threadbare trousers came up to me, looked me over with his watery grey eyes, and said, 'Sir, would you like to buy some gladioli bulbs?' He held up a basket full of bulbs which might have been onions. His chin was covered with a grey stubble, some of his teeth were missing, the remaining ones yellow with neglect.

'No, thanks,' I said. 'I live in a tiny flat in Delhi. No room for flowers.'

'A world without flowers,' he shook his head. 'That's what it's coming to.'

'And where do you plant your bulbs?'

'I grow gladioli, sir, and sell the bulbs to good people like you. My name's Foster. I own the lands all the way down to the waterfall.'

For a landowner he did not look very prosperous. But his name intrigued me.

'Isn't this area called Fosterganj?' I asked.

'That's right. My grandfather was the first to settle here. He was a grandson of Bonnie Prince Charlie who fought the British at Bannockburn. I'm the last Foster of Fosterganj. Are you sure you won't buy my daffodil bulbs?'

'I thought you said they were gladioli.'

'Some gladioli, some daffodils.'

They looked like onions to me, but to make him happy I parted with two rupees (which seemed the going rate in Fosterganj) and relieved him of his basket of bulbs. Foster shuffled off, looking a bit like Chaplin's tramp but not half as dapper. He clearly needed the two rupees. Which made me feel less foolish about spending money that I should have held on to. Writers were poor in those days. Though I didn't feel poor.

Back at the tea shop I asked Melaram if Foster really owned a lot of land.

'He has a broken-down cottage and the right-of-way. He charges people who pass through his property. Spends all the money on booze. No one owns the hillside, it's government land. Reserved forest. But everyone builds on it.'

Just as well, I thought, as I returned to town with my basket of onions. Who wanted another noisy hill station? One Mall Road was more than enough. Back in my hotel room, I was about to throw the bulbs away, but on second thoughts decided to keep them. After all, even an onion makes a handsome plant.

◆

Keep right on to the end of the road,
Keep right on to the end.
If your way be long
Let your heart be strong,
And keep right on to the end.
If you're tired and weary
Still carry on,
Till you come to your happy abode.
And then all you love
And are dreaming of,
Will be there—
At the end of the road!

The voice of Sir Harry Lauder, Scottish troubadour of the 1930s, singing one of his favourites, came drifting across the hillside as I took the winding path to Foster's cottage.

On one of my morning walks, I had helped him round up some runaway hens, and he had been suitably grateful.

'Ah, it's a fowl subject, trying to run a poultry farm,' he quipped. 'I've already lost a few to jackals and foxes. Hard to keep them in their pens. They jump over the netting and wander all over the place. But thank you for your help. It's good to be young. Once the knees go, you'll never be young again. Why don't you come over in the evening and split a bottle with me? It's a home-made brew, can't hurt you.'

I'd heard of Foster's home-made brew. More than one person had tumbled down the khad after partaking of the stuff. But I did not want to appear standoffish, and besides, I was curious about the man and his history. So towards sunset one summer's evening, I took the path down to his cottage, following the strains of Harry Lauder.

The music grew louder as I approached, and I had to knock on the door several times before it was opened by my bleary-eyed host. He had already been at the stuff he drank, and at first he failed to recognize me.

'Nice old song you have there,' I said. 'My father used to sing it when I was a boy.'

Recognition dawned, and he invited me in. 'Come in, laddie, come in. I've been expecting you. Have a seat!'

The seat he referred to was an old sofa and it was occupied by three cackling hens. With a magnificent sweep of the arm Foster swept them away, and they joined two other hens and a cock-bird on a book rack at the other end of the room.

I made sure there were no droppings on the sofa before subsiding into it.

'Birds are finding it too hot out in the yard,' he explained. 'Keep wanting to come indoors.'

The gramophone record had run its course, and Foster switched off the old record player.

'Used to have a real gramophone,' he said, 'but can't get the needles any more. These electric players aren't any good. But I still have all the old records.' He indicated a pile of 78 rpm gramophone records, and I stretched across and sifted through some of them. Gracie Fields, George Formby, The Street Singer...music hall favourites from the 1930s and 40s. Foster hadn't added to his collection for twenty years.

He must have been close to eighty, almost twice my age. Like his stubble (a permanent feature), the few wisps of hair on his sunburnt head were also grey. Mud had dried on his hands. His old patched-up trousers were held up by braces. There were buttons missing from his shirt, laces missing from his shoes.

'What will you have to drink, laddie? Tea, cocoa or whisky?'

'Er—not cocoa. Tea, maybe—oh, anything will do.'

'That's the spirit. Go for what you like. I make my own whisky, of course. Real Scotch from the Himalaya. I get the best barley from yonder village.' He gestured towards the next mountain, then turned to a sagging mantelpiece, fetched a bottle that contained an oily yellow liquid, and poured a generous amount into a cracked china mug. He poured a similar amount into a dirty glass tumbler, handed it to me, and said, 'Cheers! Bottoms up!'

'Bottoms up!' I said, and took a gulp.

It wasn't bad. I drank some more and asked Foster how the poultry farm was doing.

'Well, I had fifty birds to start with. But they keep wandering off, and the boys from the village make off with them. I'm down to forty. Sold a few eggs, though. Gave the bank manager the first lot. He seemed pleased. Would you like a few eggs? There's a couple on that cushion, newly laid.'

The said cushion was on a stool a few feet from me. Two large hens' eggs were supported upon it.

'Don't sit on 'em,' said Foster, letting out a cackle which was meant to be laughter. 'They might hatch!'

I took another gulp of Foster's whisky and considered the eggs again. They looked much larger now, more like goose eggs.

Everything was looking larger.

I emptied the glass and stood up to leave.

'Don't go yet,' said Foster. 'You haven't had a proper drink. And there's dinner to follow. Sausages and mash! I make my own sausages, did you know? My sausages were famous all over Mussoorie. I supplied the Savoy, Hakman's, the schools.'

'Why did you stop?' I was back on the sofa, holding another glass of Himalayan Scotch.

'Somebody started spreading a nasty rumour that I was using dog's meat. Now why would I do that when pork was cheap? Of course, during the war years a lot of rubbish went into sausages—stuff you'd normally throw away. That's why they were called "sweet mysteries". You remember the old song? "Ah! Sweet Mystery of Life!" Nebon Eddy and Jeanette Macdonald. Well, the troops used to sing it whenever they were given sausages for breakfast. You never knew what went into them—cats, dogs, camels, scorpions. If you survived those sausages, you survived the war!'

'And your sausages, what goes into them?'

'Good, healthy chicken meat. Not crow's meat, as some jealous rivals tried to make out.'

He frowned into his china mug. It was suddenly quieter inside. The hens had joined their sisters in the backyard; they were settling down for the night, sheltering in cardboard cartons and old mango-wood boxes. Quck-quck-quck. Another day nearer to having their sad necks wrung.

I looked around the room. A threadbare carpet. Walls that hadn't received a coat of paint for many years. A couple of loose rafters letting in a blast of cold air. Some pictures here and there—mostly racing scenes. Foster must have been a betting man. Perhaps that was how he ran out of money.

He noticed my interest in the pictures and said, 'Owned a racehorse once. A beauty, she was. That was in Meerut, just before the war. Meerut had a great racecourse. Races every Saturday. Punters came from Delhi. There was money to be made!'

'Did you win any?' I asked.

'Won a couple of races hands down. Then unexpectedly she came in last, and folks lost a lot of money. I had to leave town in a hurry. All my jockey's fault—he was hand in glove with the bookies. They made a killing, of course! Anyway, I sold the horse to a sporting Parsi gentleman and went into the canteen business with my Uncle Fred in Roorkee. That's Uncle Fred, up there.'

Foster gestured towards the mantelpiece. I expected to see a photograph of his Uncle Fred but instead of a photo I found myself staring at a naked skull. It was a well-polished skull and it glistened in the candlelight.

'That's Uncle Fred,' said Foster proudly.

'That skull? Where's the rest of him?'

'In his grave, back in Roorkee.'

'You mean you kept the skull but not the skeleton?'

'Well, it's a long story,' said Foster, 'but to keep it short, Uncle Fred died suddenly of a mysterious malady—a combination of brain fever, blood-pressure and housemaid's knee.'

'Housemaid's knee!'

'Yes, swollen kneecaps, brought about by being beaten too frequently with police lathis. He wasn't really a criminal, but he'd get into trouble from time to time, harmless little swindles such as printing his own lottery tickets or passing forged banknotes. Spent some time in various district jails until his health broke down. Got a pauper's funeral—but his cadaver was in demand. The students from the local medical college got into the cemetery one night and made off with his cranium! Not that he had much by way of a brain, but he had a handsome, well-formed skull, as you can see.'

I did see. And the skull appeared to be listening to the yarn, because its toothless jaws were extended in a grin; or so I fancied.

'And how did you get it back?' I asked.

'Broke into their demonstration room, naturally. I was younger then, and pretty agile. There it was on a shelf, among a lot of glass containers of alcohol, preserving everything from giant tapeworms to Ghulam Qadir's penis and testicles.'

'Ghulam Qadir?'

'Don't you know your history? He was the fellow who blinded the Emperor Shah Alam. They caught up with him near Saharanpur and cut his balls off. Preserved them for posterity. Waste of alcohol, though. Have another drink, laddie. And then for a sausage. Ah! Sweet Mystery of Life!'

After another drink and several 'mystery' sausages, I made my getaway and stumbled homewards up a narrow path along an open ridge. A jackal slunk ahead of me, and a screech owl screeched, but I got home safely, none the worse for an evening with the descendant of Bonnie Prince Charlie.

REMEMBER THIS DAY

If you can get an entire year off from school when you are nine years old, and can have a memorable time with a great father, then that year has to be the best time of your life even if it is followed by sorrow and insecurity.

It was the result of my parents' separation at a time when my father was on active service in the RAF during World War II. He managed to keep me with him for a summer and winter, at various locations in New Delhi—Hailey Road, Atul Grove Lane, Scindia House—in apartments he had rented, as he was not permitted to keep a child in the quarters assigned to service personnel. This arrangement suited me perfectly, and I had a wonderful year in Delhi, going to the cinema, quaffing milkshakes, helping my father with his stamp collection; but this idyllic situation could not continue forever, and when my father was transferred to Karachi he had no option but to put me in a boarding school.

This was the Bishop Cotton Preparatory School in Simla—or rather, Chhota Simla—where boys studied up to Class 4, after which they moved on to the senior school.

Although I was a shy boy, I had settled down quite well in

the friendly atmosphere of this little school, but I did miss my father's companionship, and I was overjoyed when he came up to see me during the midsummer break. He had a couple of days' leave, and he could only take me out for a day, bringing me back to school in the evening.

I was so proud of him when he turned up in his dark blue RAF uniform, a flight lieutenant's stripes very much in evidence as he had just been promoted.

He was already forty, engaged in Codes and Ciphers and not flying much. He was short and stocky, getting bald, but smart in his uniform. I gave him a salute—I loved giving salutes—and he returned the salutation and followed it up with a hug and a kiss on my forehead.

'And what would you like to do today, son?'

'Let's go to Davico's,' I said.

Davico's was the best restaurant in town, famous for its meringues, marzipans, curry puffs and pastries. So to Davico's we went, where of course I gorged myself on confectionery as only a small schoolboy can do.

'Lunch is still a long way off, so let's take a walk,' suggested my father.

And provisioning ourselves with more pastries, we left the Mall and trudged up to the Monkey Temple at the top of Jakko Hill. Here we were relieved of the pastries by the monkeys, who simply snatched them away from my unwilling hands, and we came downhill in a hurry before I could get hungry again. Small boys and monkeys have much in common.

My father suggested a rickshaw ride around Elysium Hill, and this we did in style, swept along by four sturdy young rickshaw-pullers. My father took the opportunity of relating the story of Kipling's 'Phantom Rickshaw' (this was before I discovered it in print), and a couple of other ghost stories designed to build up my appetite for lunch.

We ate at Wenger's (or was it Clark's?) and then—

'Enough of ghosts, Ruskin. Let's go to the pictures.'

I loved going to the pictures. I know the Delhi cinemas intimately, and it hadn't taken me long to discover the Simla cinemas. There were three of them—the Regal, the Ritz and the Rivoli.

We went to the Rivoli. It was down near the ice-skating rink and the old Blessington Hotel. The film was about an ice-skater and starred Sonja Henie, a pretty young Norwegian Olympic champion who appeared in a number of Hollywood musicals. All she had to do was skate and look pretty, and this she did to perfection. I decided to fall in love with her. But by the time I grew up and finished school she'd stopped skating and making films! Whatever happened to Sonja Henie?

After the picture it was time to return to school. We walked all the way to Chhota Simla talking about what we'd do during the winter holidays, and where we would go when the war was over.

'I'll be in Calcutta now,' said my father. 'There are good bookshops there. And cinemas. And Chinese restaurants. And we'll buy more gramophone records, and add to the stamp collection.'

It was dusk when we walked slowly down the path to the school gate and playing-field. Two of my friends were waiting for me—Bimal and Riaz. My father spoke to them, asked about their homes. A bell started ringing.

We said goodbye.

'Remember this day, Ruskin,' said my father.

He patted me gently on the head and walked away.

I never saw him again.

Three months later I heard that he had passed away in the

military hospital in Calcutta.

I dream of him sometimes, and in my dream he is always the same, caring for me and leading me by the hand along old familiar roads.

And of course I remember that day. Over sixty-five years have passed, but it's as fresh as yesterday.

AN EVENING AT THE SAVOY WITH H.H.*

H.H. back in town meant that Signor Montalban was back too, and for the convenience of all concerned it was decided that his family would move into the rented house selected for them. Pablo did not object to the move, as the house was nearer to the town and its cinemas. It meant that I would see less of them as my cottage was almost an hour's walk in the opposite direction.

Montalban's visits to Mussoorie to see his beloved were brief, and he spent more time at the Hollow Oak palace than at his wife's residence. H.H. threw a party whenever he was in town. Mrs Montalban, pleading indisposition, stayed away. I attended only one of them, a lugubrious affair which ended with Neena drinking too much and ending up, quite literally, under the table. In trying to extricate her, I too collapsed on the floor, and we ended up a tangle of arms and legs.

'Just like old times,' said Neena, subsiding into a sofa. 'I wish you had got to grips with me when we were a little younger.'

---

*From *Maharani*

'I did try,' I said. 'But you were always as elusive as a shark. You were looking for other prey.'

'Well, you were rather dull. Always had your head in a book. But I hear you're quite friendly with that equally dull creature, Signora Montalban.'

'She likes books too,' I said. 'I lend her mine and she lends me hers.'

'How romantic. Like Elizabeth Barrett and Robert Browning, reading their poems to each other.'

'Bet you never read any of their poetry.' 'Yes, I did. At school, remember? "The Pied Piper of Hamelin". And you're a bit of a Pied Piper yourself. That boy follows you around everywhere.'

'Pablo. He needs a father. But his father doesn't need him. Too busy elsewhere. Too busy mixing drinks.'

Montalban was doing just that—standing behind H.H.'s minibar, making drinks for her guests.

'Diplomatic duties,' I said.

'You're just jealous,' said Neena.

'And you're just jealous of Elizabeth Barrett Browning.'

Neena gave a shriek of laughter, got up, and sat down on the floor again. This time I did not help her up, but left her to the attentions of a tall, strikingly handsome foreigner wearing a saffron robe. It turned out that he was an Anglo-German neophyte at an ashram up in the mountains. He was drinking apple juice.

◆

Mrs Montalban moved into her new abode without any fuss or bother, engaged a cook and a maidservant, and directed all her energies into caring for her children. In other words, she was the ideal Indian wife and mother.

So, while H.H. played the femme fatale and Montalban

fancied himself a Valentino, Mrs Montalban was simply a homely bread-and-butter woman who busied herself baking cakes and cookies.

And she baked them well, as I discovered one afternoon when I dropped in at Pablo's invitation a week or two after they had moved into their new abode.

Already, the wide veranda looked like no veranda I had ever seen. The walls were festooned with film posters, all assiduously collected over the summer months. Apart from the manager of the Picture Palace, Pablo had made friends with the projectionist at the Rialto, the ticket seller at the Majestic, and the tea stall owner at the Jubilee—all of whom had gone out of their way to save posters for him. Partly it was due to his personal charm and friendly nature; partly due to his generosity with his mother's cakes and cookies.

And now, on my first visit to the rented house, I was taken from one poster to another as though I were the chief guest at a grand art exhibition—which is what it was, in a way. For here were the great stars of the sixties and earlier in some of their most famous roles. And Pablo, in a way, was a pioneer, for he had discovered that the film poster was an art form in itself, and I doubt if anyone, till then, had built up such a collection. He must have had close to a hundred posters. Not all were on the veranda wall. His favourites were in his bedroom. And when I went to the bathroom to ease myself, I found myself staring at a large poster of *It's a Mad Mad Mad Mad World*. And I had to agree with it.

It was little sister Anna's birthday.

A large cake stood on a table in the sunroom—a small sitting room with glazed window. During the day it received the morning sun; at night, the rising moon. It was Anna's favourite room, and she liked to sit there and draw or paint until it grew dark.

I looked at some of her sketches—flower studies, trees, small animals—all quite charming but nothing out of the ordinary—until I came to a sketch of a face, just a line drawing, incomplete but in a way quite compelling; the face of a girl, pretty and vivacious, but a little old-fashioned, judging by the plaited hair and the ribbons.

'Who's this?' I asked.

'Just a girl I saw the other day. She looked at me over the gate and hurried away. It was raining. I saw her again yesterday. She had her face pressed to the window. She looked very sweet, but shy like a gazelle—she had her face against the glass and she kept staring at me. That's how I remember her features so well. But when I got up to open the window, she ran off. Just disappeared! I hope she comes again. I'd like her for a friend.'

I was the only guest at that little birthday party. Mrs Montalban had met a number of people while staying at Hollow Oak, but they had all been Neena's friends; she hadn't hit it off with any of them. Her English was weak and her Hindi non-existent; she spoke to her children in Spanish. But she was aware of Pablo's growing affection for me and she was glad of any overtures of friendship towards her and her family.

Montalban was of course absent—out of town—away on a diplomatic mission to Thailand or Timbuctoo, and this time without H.H. for company.

The cake was splendid, full of good things like walnuts and raisins and cherries, and I have to confess that I consumed the lion's share; but I was always like that, a glutton for the good things in life—birthday cakes, books and a comfortable bed, all in that order. Mrs M and the children were delighted by my appetite, and Mrs M vowed to bake bigger and better cakes if I would come over more often. I promised that I would.

H.H. must have heard that it was Anna's birthday because

presently one of her lackeys arrived with a large gift-wrapped parcel. When opened, it revealed an expensive doll, beautifully dressed, with what appeared to be a real hair—glossy black tresses—done up in a coiffure. Anna stood it up on the table and it immediately broke into a chorus of 'Happy Birthday to you!'

We all clapped and Mrs Montalban sat down to write a thank you note to Neena. She would have sent her some cake too, but for the fact that I had finished it.

Pablo was staring intently at the doll.

'It looks like the maharani,' he said, a glint of the devil in his eyes.

'Even the voice is a bit like hers,' I added.

'It's a beautiful doll,' said Mrs Montalban. 'Especially the dress.'

'And the hair,' said Anna, stroking it gently.

The doll was put aside and Pablo produced a guitar and began strumming on it.

'I didn't know you could play the guitar,' I said.

'Only a little bit,' he said, and played a familiar tune which sounded a bit like 'Jealousy', a tango from an earlier time. The tune was perhaps a fitting prelude to what happened next.

There was a jingle of bells and a rickshaw pulled by two uniformed but barefooted young men pulled up at the gate, and out stepped H.H. in all her finery, looking very regal, albeit a little unsteady on her feet.

'A party without me,' she scolded, genuinely upset. 'Why didn't you invite me?'

'It was just the children,' said Mrs Montalban defensively.

'And I suppose you're Peter Pan,' said Neena, glaring at me.

'I thought I was supposed to be the Pied Piper,' I said. 'But I came accidentally. I didn't know it was Anna's birthday.'

'It's just like the maharani,' said Pablo, straight-faced. 'Even the voice.'

Neena ignored him. She had been conscious of his resentment ever since she had seduced his father. It did not bother her. Spreading a little unhappiness was one of her chief pleasures.

'Well,' she said, hands on hips, a typical pose when she wanted to get her way. 'We're going to celebrate properly. No tea and cakes, just cakes and ale! I'm taking you out for dinner. We'll go to the Savoy! And you can come too, Pied Piper. A pity Ricardo isn't here, but you'll have to do as our escort or whatever.'

'Your friend in need,' I said. 'Always at your service.'

'Good. You can pay for the drinks.'

The rickshaw—the late maharaja's personal rickshaw—was dismissed as it could only seat two. Rickshaws were on their way out and only a few remained in town. But there were now three taxis and we sent for one of them, a large Chevrolet which had seen better days. I sat up front next to the driver and H.H., and Mrs Montalban and the children squeezed in at the back.

It was late July, and a monsoon mist hung over the mountain. There were hardly any tourists in town and the grand old hotel was practically empty; but the bar was functioning, or so it seemed, and Neena headed straight for it.

Like the rickshaw and the taxi and the royal house of Mastipur, the old hotel had also seen better days. A musty odour emanated from the worn carpets. Outside it was raining; but inside, the decorative plants were drooping from lack of water. If you sat on an easy chair in the lounge there was a strong possibility of a loose spring probing your rectum.

H.H. wasn't wasting time in the lounge. She headed straight for the bar. She barged through the swing doors and we were immediately assailed by the combined odour of stale beer, mildew and disintegrating cheese-and-tomato sandwiches.

Neena herded us into this chamber of horrors and called out, 'Barman, barman, beer for all!'

There was no response.

The room was empty and there was no one behind the bar.

'Perhaps it's a dry day,' I said. 'Or someone's death anniversary.'

'Shut up,' said Neena. 'There are no dry days in this town.' She peered over the bar counter, then let out a shriek of laughter. 'Maybe there's a death after all. Our bartender is well and truly pissed!'

True enough, the bartender was stretched out on the floor, snoring away, blissfully unaware of the arrival of customers. It was obvious he'd been helping himself to various liquors and liqueurs, trying each one for taste and aroma.

'He's completely blotto,' said Neena. 'We'll just have to help ourselves.' And she reached for a bottle of Scotch, intoning. 'Don't be vague. Ask for Haig.'

'A glass of wine for me,' interposed Mrs Montalban. 'The children can have soft drinks.'

'No soft drinks here,' said Neena. 'But Pablo can have a beer. My boys started when they were six.'

'No lip from you, Peter Piper. Down your whisky and then go in search of the manager. If you can't find the manager, find the cook. If you can't find the cook, find the masalchi. We want something to eat. It's Anna's birthday, damn and blast!'

Damned and blasted, I went in search of the hotel staff and, after wandering around the empty halls and corridors of this vast mausoleum, finally bumped into someone who looked like a manager.

'We're looking for something to eat,' I said.

'Well, so am I, sir.'

'Are you the manager?'

'No, I'm the pianist.'

'Pianist! But I haven't seen a piano anywhere.' '[T]here['s no] one. They sold it last week to a collector from Bo[mbay]. Ivan Lobo,' he said, extending his hand.

We shook hands and I introduced myself.

'The hotel appears to be deserted,' I said. 'And the [bartender] is fast asleep.'

'Well, the hotel is up for sale, you know. The owne[r is] missing—last seen in Bangladesh. And the cook is i[n hospital] with food poisoning.'

'Well, in that case, I don't think we'll want anythi[ng to eat.] I'd better go back to the bar and tell the others.'

'I'll come with you,' said Mr Lobo. 'Perhaps I can b[e of help.]'

When we got to the bar, Neena was on her secon[d drink.]

'Don't be vague,' she chirruped. 'Ask for Haig!'

'This is Mr Lobo,' I said. 'He's the pianist.'

'How lovely! It's just the sort of evening for some [piano] music. 'What Do They Do On a Rainy Night in Ri[o?' Play] that one.'

'Well, it's a rainy night in Mussoorie. And there's [no piano.] And no cook.'

'Well, fetch the owner. Isn't he around?'

'He's gone underground,' I said.

'Oh, it's old Chawla, I am not surprised. Used to pla[y cards] with my husband. Did nothing else. Have a drink, [Mr Lobo,] I've always had a soft spot for pianists.'

She poured Mr Lobo a Patiala peg and gave hersel[f one.] Meanwhile, the bartender had woken from his slum[ber,] wiped his face on a tablecloth, burped, and asked u[s if we'd] like something to drink.

...ithout you,' said Neena. 'But give ...man. You look as though you need ...e out of job next week.'

... said Mr Lobo, expanding a little ...of Haig. 'We have to do something ...ourself together, run down to the ...d from the Hum Tum Dhaba. What

... Your Highness. I didn't know you ...icture in the papers. The Maharani

...m unfamiliar with the names of so

...laying the piano in Goa? Everyone

...i Hendrix died in his bathtub and ...ose. Singers get nervous when they ...ven. That's when they succumb to

..., not a singer. And if you're out of ...lay the piano for me every evening.

...n.'

...m the Hum Tum Dhaba (at Savoy ...I tucked in. Mrs Montalban never ate ...on the whisky. And Mr Lobo, out of ...s. The taxi having been dismissed, the bartender was sent out in search of another, but failed to return.

The evening had been too much for him.

The clock on the wall hadn't worked since the great earthquake of 1905, but my watch was showing midnight when the party broke up. Mrs Montalban and the children decided to walk home. Neena was by now incapable of walking. Mr Lobo and I got her as far as the front steps, where she subsided into a hydrangea bush.

'There's an old rickshaw kept in a shed near the office,' said Mr Lobo. 'I'll see if I can get someone to pull it for us.'

But at that late hour there was no rickshaw-puller to be found. I was still trying to extricate Neena from the hydrangea—and being roundly abused in the process—when Mr Lobo came round the corner, pulling the decrepit but movable rickshaw.

'If you can get her in,' he gasped, already out of breath, 'we'll take her home ourselves!'

'He's a real man!' shrieked Neena. 'Not a namby-pamby bastard like you!'

'Any more abuse and I'll leave you here with Mr Lobo. You can both occupy the VIP suite. Many famous people have slept in it—Emperor Haile Selassie, the Panchen Lama, Pearl S. Buck, Raj Kapoor, Helen, and Polly Umrigar the cricketer.'

'What—all together?' giggled Neena. 'It must have been quite an orgy!'

'Not all together, Your Highness. Separately, and at different times.'

'Helen of Troy, too.'

'Not Helen of Troy. Helen, the Bollywood dancer.'

'Well then, let's dance,' said H.H., making a great effort to get up. 'Mr Lobo can play the piano while we dance.'

'First we have to get you home. The piano's at your place, remember? The hotel doesn't have one.'

'When We're all out Dancing Cheek to Cheek,' H.H. began singing an old Fred Astaire number.

Mr Lobo and I began singing along with her, at the same time getting her to stand up and stagger towards the rickshaw. We managed to get her on to the seat, where she sat up for a moment, observing, 'These two don't look like my rickshaw boys,' before subsiding again.

'You pull and I'll push,' said Mr Lobo gallantly.

'No, you pull and I'll push,' I countered. 'Pulling is better exercise for piano players. I'm just a pen-pusher.'

That settled, we set off on the long haul to Hollow Oak, and believe me, it was a struggle all the way. The rickshaw was an old one, long out of use. It squeaked and rattled, and the wheels gave every indication of wanting to come off. Nevertheless, we made progress, encouraged by cries of abuse alternating with shouts of merriment from H.H., who was obviously enjoying the ride.

For those few who were out on the Mall that night, it must have been quite a sight—Kipling's phantom rickshaw emerging from the mist on a moonlit night, propelled along by a couple of well-dressed but dishevelled gentlemen who were spurred on by a mad maharani waving in royal fashion to an imaginary crowd—the effect spoilt only by the obscenities that tripped off her tongue.

We got her home eventually and put her to bed. I had the guest room opened for Mr Lobo and told him he'd better stay the night.

'About giving me a job as a pianist,' he said. 'Did she really mean it?'

'You'll know in the morning,' I said. 'Get a good night's sleep. And if she throws you out in the morning, you can come and have breakfast with me.'

'Well, so am I, sir.'

'Are you the manager?'

'No, I'm the pianist.'

'Pianist! But I haven't seen a piano anywhere.' 'There isn't one. They sold it last week to a collector from Bombay. I'm Ivan Lobo,' he said, extending his hand.

We shook hands and I introduced myself.

'The hotel appears to be deserted,' I said. 'And the bartender is fast asleep.'

'Well, the hotel is up for sale, you know. The owner has gone missing—last seen in Bangladesh. And the cook is in hospital with food poisoning.'

'Well, in that case, I don't think we'll want anything to eat. I'd better go back to the bar and tell the others.'

'I'll come with you,' said Mr Lobo. 'Perhaps I can be of help.'

When we got to the bar, Neena was on her second whisky.

'Don't be vague,' she chirruped. 'Ask for Haig!'

'This is Mr Lobo,' I said. 'He's the pianist.'

'How lovely! It's just the sort of evening for some romantic music. "What Do They Do On a Rainy Night in Rio?" I love that one.'

'Well, it's a rainy night in Mussoorie. And there's no piano. And no cook.'

'Well, fetch the owner. Isn't he around?'

'He's gone underground,' I said.

'Oh, it's old Chawla, I am not surprised. Used to play billiards with my husband. Did nothing else. Have a drink, Mr Lobo. I've always had a soft spot for pianists.'

She poured Mr Lobo a Patiala peg and gave herself another. Meanwhile, the bartender had woken from his slumbers. He wiped his face on a tablecloth, burped, and asked us if we'd like something to drink.

'We're doing all right without you,' said Neena. 'But give yourself a drink, you poor man. You look as though you need one. And you'll probably be out of job next week.'

'Now then, Melaram,' said Mr Lobo, expanding a little under the gentle influence of Haig. 'We have to do something for our guests here. Pull yourself together, run down to the bazaar, and order some food from the Hum Tum Dhaba. What would like madam?'

'Maharani, no madam.'

'A thousand pardons, Your Highness. I didn't know you were you. I've seen your picture in the papers. The Maharani of Ranipur.'

'Mastipur, sir. Mastipur.

'Coming from Goa, I am unfamiliar with the names of so many of our states.'

'So why aren't you playing the piano in Goa? Everyone there is a musician, I hear.'

'They were, until Jimi Hendrix died in his bathtub and Janis Joplin took an overdose. Singers get nervous when they reach the age of twenty-seven. That's when they succumb to something or the other.'

'Well, you're a pianist, not a singer. And if you're out of a job, you can come and play the piano for me every evening. It needs tuning anyway.'

'Much obliged, ma'am.'

'Maharani ji.'

'Your Highness.'

'That's better.'

Food was brought from the Hum Tum Dhaba (at Savoy prices) and the children and I tucked in. Mrs Montalban never ate much. H.H. concentrated on the whisky. And Mr Lobo, out of politeness, kept pace with us. The taxi having been dismissed, the